TOO SKINT TO OD

TOO SKINT TO OD

A Long Time Ago in a Glasgow Scheme
Far Far Away

Joe Reavey

Too Skint To OD

A Long Time Ago in a Glasgow Scheme Far Far Away

© 2025 Joe Reavey

This is a work of fiction. Names, characters, places, and
incidents are either the product of the author's imagination
or are used fictitiously. Any resemblance to actual persons,
living or dead, events, or locales is entirely coincidental.

ISBNs:

eBook: 978-1-80541-781-1
Paperback: 978-1-80541-782-8

TABLE OF CONTENTS

For Ann, the best mother
a rascal of a son could ask for...

AUTHOR'S NOTE

The characters in this book are not based on one person. They are fictional characters taken from guys I have known my whole life, from school to work and in pubs. The Crow is taken from one of my old pals whose nickname was the Crow. I always thought it was a cool badass nickname and we both talked about if ever I did a book the bad guy would be called the Crow.

This is a story about three young guys growing up in Glasgow in the nineties, experiencing everything from drugs and drink to love and loss, having nothing but their friendship to help them get by. Working, begging and stealing cash for the weekend thinking it would never end and facing the fact that life will skip past you in the blink of an eye.

CHAPTER 1

PALS...

One minute you're eighteen, getting your end away and getting higher than a giraffe's fanny. Next you're fifty and the only pills you buy are from Holland and Barrett. Well, let's go back to the good old days when the music was so good it explained how you felt in life. The days before Wi-Fi, Facebook and mobile phones in our pockets like tags round our fucking ankles. Back to the days when the winters were cold but the summers lasted forever.

The sun was shining in a clear Glasgow sky and Jagger was feeling good about the day ahead with his pals. It was pay day for them. Well, wages day for Jagger and giro day for Ringo and Syd. This only happened once every two weeks as they only got their dole money every second week. He was feeling good about meeting his pals knowing that they had money in their pockets to spend unlike every other week when they would meet up and just get drunk on his money.

He left the hot heat of the summer sun and walked into the dark pub. It was busy with all the same old faces, all the same guys hiding from their wives who were all at home waiting to take their wages off them. He squeezed through the crowd and the smoke looking for his pals in the dark busy pub. It was like a Vegas hotel. You couldn't tell what time it was. Maybe that was to make you stay longer. It was so dark that some of the old guys had been in there that long if they went out into that summer sun they would fucking blow up like a wee drunk vampire.

"Jagger, over here," Ringo shouted waving like a mad man happy to see his pal.

They were all named after guys from their favourite bands. They were the only guys in the pub who weren't into football. For them it was about getting stoned and getting the tunes on the jukebox, so some smart cunt in the pub gave them their nicknames.

"All right, lads, how's things?"

Syd looked up, smiled and said, "Thank fuck you're here. This cunt is doing my nut in talking shit."

"No I'm no'. I was just asking him who is his favourite superhero is."

"And I told you," snapped Syd, "It's fucking Batman."

Ringo laughed. "Batman isn't a superhero. He is a vigilante. He takes the law into his own hands."

Jagger sat down handing out the beer and the smokes. "Right, my turn. It's fucking Superman. He is the most powerful out of any of them. He is the Hobnob of the biscuit family. That cunt Batman he is more a chocolate Penguin."

"No, he fights the Penguin."

"Well, whatever. Superman is the main man of superheroes end of."

Syd asked, "How does he get his powers again?"

Ringo chipped in, "From eating Hobnobs apparently."

"Funny cunt. No, he gets it from the sun I'm sure."

Syd said, "Well, he wouldn't be much good in Scotland, would he?"

"No," Jagger laughed, "He would only be able to fight bad guys two weeks in July when the sun shows up. The rest of the time he would be getting the shit kicked out of him in the dull pissing rain."

"Ok, wait a minute. Right, Ringo, I hate to ask but who is your favourite superhero? This I got to hear."

"Wolverine."

Jagger and Syd burst out laughing.

"Fuck off," Jagger said.

"No, hear me out. Think about it. He drinks whisky and beers, he smokes the best cigars, Cuban probably, and he never gets old and fat."

"Like you," Syd said laughing.

"And he gets all the birds. No' a bad life if you ask me, guys."

Jagger was having none of it. "No, mate. That's all Hollywood bullshit. Drink beer and still have a six pack?

And anyway it would be a nightmare being him. He could never go on holiday."

"How?" Ringo asked.

"Because he would never get them big fucking claws through security."

"Yeah, fuck that," Syd said, "Everyone needs two weeks in Spain now and then."

Jagger put his empty glass on the table. Right, boys. Whose turn is it to hit the bar?"

Ringo said, "I will get them in."

Jagger asked him if he would like a map.

"No, mate. I'm sure I will find it."

"Might need a flashlight. It's like the fucking Batcave in here."

"Maybe that's why Syd loves it in here."

Jagger asked, "Syd, you get your dole money today?"

"Yes, mate, I did. Seventy-three pounds for the next two weeks. Fucking shit. And the government wonders why we sell drugs. They forget we need to eat."

"Aye," Jagger said, "We all need our bit on the side, mate."

"Don't let your Sally hear you saying that. She will cut your fucking nuts off, mate."

"No, you know what I mean. A wee bit of extra money. No pussy. I'm happy with what I've got. Anyway, talking of birds, is Daisy coming in tonight because Sally's popping in later."

"Aye, she should be in at some point. She is away to the bingo with her ma. Hopefully she wins the full house and all our money problems will be over."

Jagger said, "If she wins, mate, you'll be single faster than I can shout house. Never mind a full house."

Ringo came back over with the beers.

Jagger said to him, "Take it you got your dole money today too?"

"Yes, I did. Or as I like to call it: my giro beer tokens. And I have a wee extra five hundred bucks too," he replied with a smile on his face.

"Ok, we're listening," Syd said.

"Well, I was in here last week talking to see Tam Stewart who works in the dole office and is brand new with us. Well, anyway he was telling me how he has been struggling to sell his house."

"Where does he stay?" Jagger asked.

"Just round the corner from your uncle Jim, Syd. You know just beside the Bull Dog Inn."

"That's a shithole of an area," said Syd, "That pub should be called the House of the Rising Sun. It's full of bad cunts all gambling and stabbing. He will never get a good price for his house."

"Well, he did thanks to me," said Ringo. "I told him I would get it sold not only for a good price but sold fast too."

"So how did you do it?"

"Well, as luck would have it, I knew the guy next door to Tam, wee Jimmy. I worked with him a few years ago. Anyway, I asked him if I could bring some birds round for a wee drink out his back. You know, enjoy this lovely weather we are having and what with wee Jimmy choking for a bird and thinking he might get his hole… well, he was right up for it. So I got hold of the twins who work in the kebab shop. You know, that shithole. The kebabs are shit but every cunt still goes in just for the twins."

"I was in last night," said Syd.

"Yeah, well, I gave them fifty pounds each to come along for a drink and a dip in the paddling pool and it was the every same day that wee Tam had his house viewing. I'm no' kidding. The first couple to show up the guy was out the back hanging over the fence trying to get a good look at the twins and he wasn't asking questions about the fucking gaff. No, it was all questions like, 'So are yous girls over here a lot?" And they were standing there all wet in their wee bikinis saying, 'Yeah, we don't have a back garden so we come over here to get some sun.' Every time a new couple showed up the guy was always right out the back. By the end of the day, wee Tam had five good offers on the house and I was up five hundred pounds. So I got us a big bag of coke to do us all weekend, boys. Let the weekend begin."

As they were laughing and drinking, the door burst open and the sunshine blinded all the pub, making everyone want to look away. It was four guys, three big guys and one small guy. It was the Crow and his back-up.

The Crow was the drug dealer in the scheme and no cunt fucked with him. He dressed smart and you could tell he had a bit of money and he didn't care who knew. He had jet-black hair and dark eyes like a young Ronnie Wood and that's how he got his nickname: the Crow. From the side he had the look of a raven. He knew that Ringo and the boys sold a bit but most of it they got from him so he didn't mind. The Crow was a loud and in your face kind of guy but no one had a problem with him because if they did he would slash them or his back-up would so he could do whatever he wanted.

"All right, ladies. What's happening? You out for a wee shandy?"

"You're the one who drinks lager tops, no' us," said Ringo.

"Fuck up, wee man, no cunt was asking you and anyway you're that hard up for a bird your pals have to get you a hooker for your birthday every year."

"No, they don't," said Ringo with shame in his eyes.

"Yes, they fucking do. Last year they paid Fat Ammo to suck you off round the back of the pub. I mean, imagine paying to play hide the sausage with that fat cow. Did you ever have a wee threesome with her and her fat boyfriend Dell the Smell?"

Dell the smell was the local hash head and junkie who was always bragging when he should have been begging because he had fuck all. He drove a shit heap of a car but had a Ferrari key ring. Everyone knew him as the smelly cunt and no one had any time for him but he would buy a lot of hash from the boys and his bird fat Annmarie was a cheap ride for sum of the guys in the pub who were hard up.

The Crow said, "Right, girls, it was lovely talking to yous. I'm away to the bar for a beer."

"Lager tops," Syd whispered.

The pub was now jumping. Everyone had that Friday feeling and were all looking forward to a good weekend away from their work. Just like every working class guy in Scotland, they lived for the weekend.

Just as the pub was in full swing and the sun was setting, the door swung open again. This time it wasn't a bunch of ugly cunts. No, it was Sally, the best looking girl in the scheme, standing there with the sun setting behind her. All eyes were on her but her eyes were only looking for her man Jagger. She walked in like she was on a catwalk heading right over to the table where the boys were. Every guy looked at Jagger thinking the same thing: *How could a big ugly cunt like him get a wee bird like that?*

Even the Crow had a soft spot for her. "It breaks my heart seeing that cunt with her," he said. "I mean, what does she see in him and his sad mates? Fucking kills me."

"Take it you like her then, boss?" one of his boys said.

The Crow got right up in his face and said, "What, can't you tell? Of fucking course I like her. That wee bird is so fit I would fuck her shadow."

Sally hugged Jagger and asked him how his day off had been.

"It was ok till I bumped into these two."

Sally asked Syd if Daisy was coming in for a drink.

"She will be in soon. She is working tonight."

Syd's girlfriend worked behind the bar twice a week for some extra cash and it suited the boys who would get a wee free pint now and then when no cunt was looking. Especially the two barmaids who ran the pub, known as Cagney and Lacey. They didn't fuck about. Anyone getting up to no good was out and you had to do a lot of begging to get back in.

If you went for a pint on a Monday you would notice a few guys hanging about waiting to see the girls to say sorry and please let them back in. Their wee office was like a confession box with every cunt waiting to go in and sell their soul for a pint of Tennent's.

At five minutes past five the door kicked open and in ran Daisy five minutes late.

As she ran past all the pissheads, one of them shouted, "Hey, hen, watch you don't boil your waters."

Daisy snapped back at him, "Don't worry. You will never burn your wee dick in anyway."

Ringo and Jagger looked at Syd and all he said was, "That girl is a keeper, lads."

Jagger had a sniff about at the table and said, "Some cunt has dropped their play peace in here. It fucking stinks."

Sally said, "I can smell it. Fucking old guy farts. I'm away to sit in the lounge and talk to Daisy."

Ringo told the boys, "I was in here last night and I'm sure that cunt Del the Smell had shit himself. He was stinking."

"We know, mate. That's why he's called Del the fucking Smell."

"I know that but last night he was out his nut and he normally smells like sweaty balls but you could tell he had done a shit in his pants. You could tell the way he was sitting. The cunt tried to sit with me but I told him to fuck off. I was wondering why he was hanging about. His fat bird was sucking some cunt off round the back of the pub. She is a dirty cow and when I was coming into the pub she was sucking off the taxi driver who had dropped them off to save her paying the fare."

Jagger said, "If I was a taxi driver I would rather have the fare and no tip. Fuck that. She is so bad an IRA sniper wouldn't take her out."

Syd agreed. "Yeah, she would be safe on a cruise ship full of horny sailors."

At the next table from them was a wee drunk guy who was asleep.

"I see wee Archie got an early finish today," said Jagger.

Ringo asked, "Is that his name? I didn't know."

"How could you not know Archie? Every cunt in here knows who he is."

"Yeah, I know him. I just didn't know his name was Archie, that's all. And maybe if he was awake longer than two pints to talk to me then I would know his name."

As the boys sat looking at the wee sleeping drunk guy in his dirty work gear, Syd said, "It's funny. I bet every pub in Scotland has a wee hard working sleeping drunk guy."

"Yeah and he is harmless until he needs a piss then the wee cunt will piss anywhere."

Jagger told them, "The last time he was trying to get into the confession box thinking it was the toilet, your Daisy was pushing him away. He was pissing everywhere like a fucking garden sprinkler. Guys were covering their pints and running for their lives."

Syd put a small bag of white power down on the table beside his pint. "Right, lads. It's time for a few Patsy Clines to get us in the mood for the night ahead."

"Sounds good to me," said Ringo, "A few lines of the old devil's dandruff then a wee Jack and Coke is just what I need after this long hard week."

Jagger laughed. "Yeah, I'm sure it was hell, mate."

Syd got up from the table and said, "See yous in about one minute and remember, play it cool. We don't need Cagney or Lacey seeing us all going for a piss at the same time."

Jagger said, "I will go last. I'll meet you in whatever cubicle doesn't smell of shit."

As the boys were huddled up together, Syd was busy chopping away fixing out three good lines.

Ringo was no' happy. "Syd, are you sure this is the best cubicle, mate? It stinks of shit."

"They all stink of shit, mate. If you don't believe me, go and have a sniff about the rest of them."

"No, I do believe you. I just hate doing lines in here. I mean, why do cunts need to shit in a pub? Can they no' do it at home like the fucking rest of us?"

Jagger told him, "They are old guys. If they pass a toilet they need to do a shit. Same as they never waste a hard-on."

As the boys took a big sniff each, Ringo looked up and said, "Fuck. Let me out, lads. I need a shit."

"You no' do that at home, Ringo?"

"Shut it and get out or I will do it in front of yous and don't be telling any cunt out there I'm shitting. And get me a Jack and Coke and lots of ice."

Jagger said to Syd, "Do you think the ice is for his hole?"

Jagger and Syd hit the bar for some drinks. "Three pints of Tennent's and three Jack Ds and Coke please."

"You all set for next week?" Syd asked.

"Hell yes, mate. I'm pretty much done. Can't wait. Four days in Benidorm with just the boys. Pure madness. Just what I need and I got my holiday insurance today."

"Do you think we will need that?"

"Well, holiday insurance is like a condom, mate. It's better to have one and no' need it than to no' have one and need it."

"True. If we don't have condoms we will end up bringing home more than just duty free."

"Yeah, fuck that and knowing yous two, we will definitely be needing holiday insurance."

"When we are away it will be Ringo's birthday."

"So what? You thinking we pack a birthday cake in our case?"

"No, I mean what will we get him?"

"The same thing we get him every year: a hooker. Just this year it will be a Spanish hooker."

As the boys took the drinks to the table Ringo came back from the toilets. "Thank fuck that's out the way. That was hard work, lads. I swear it was that big I was thinking I was in labour. I'm no' joking. And how come when you're at home and you wipe your ass it's all clean but when you're trying to do a quick shit in the pub your ass is like a seagull that's been in a fucking oil spill."

Ringo picked up his Jack and Coke and downed it in one go, then took two or three big sips of his pint. "Right, lads, whose round is it?"

"It's your fucking round, Ringo, so get to the bar."

"I know. Sorry, lads. I just want to get a few down my neck to get me in the mood and maybe find myself a wee bird tonight who has her own gaff."

"A bird and her own gaff?" laughed Jagger. "Why? You looking to get married and settle down tonight, mate?"

"No, I would just like somewhere to get my head doon because it's my ma and da's anniversary and they want the place to themself. They even sent my wee brother round to stay at my aunt Jean's and she is a fucking nightmare. Poor cunt. She will have him cleaning her house."

Jagger asked him, "Why they wanting yous all out? Is your old da going to give her one for old time's sake?"

Syd added, "Yeah, he was in here yesterday looking for some cunt to go into Ann Summers for him."

"Fuck off, yous two sick cunts. My old man hasn't got a pump left in him. He is so old fashioned he thinks a bird's clit is for turning the page in her book. No, they are just going to have a curry and watch their favourite film."

"What's that? *Basic Instinct*?"

"No, funny cunt. It's *Grease*."

"*Grease*?" the boys laugh.

"Yeah, fucking good film. First film I seen in the cinema. I think that's why it means something to them. They told me I was about five and I went up in front of the screen to dance to *Grease Lightning*."

"Well, Danny Zuko, get to the bar and get a round in and watch you don't bump into Sandy on your way back."

"Yeah, keep your 'summer loving' for next week."

Syd asked Jagger, "How was work this week, mate?"

14

"It was fucking busy. Loads of functions on but the good thing about that is it means loads of overtime and they serve alcohol at the functions so while I'm washing the pots and pans I get a few cans and some to take up the road and they give me whatever was on the menu to take home."

"That sounds no' bad. What did you take home last night?"

"Steak and pepper sauce."

"Pepper sauce? What's that? Like tomato sauce?"

"No, it's more like pepper and hot cream. You know, like rich cunts eat it.

"Sounds stinking. Fucking pepper and cream."

Ringo came back from the bar. "Who's eating cream?"

"No, Ringo. I was telling Syd about a sauce that was on the menu: steak and pepper sauce."

Ringo said, "Yeah, I'm with Syd. That sound shit."

"It's no' shit. It is one of the best sauces you can get. That's why rich cunts have it. Goes well with a sirloin or a chicken breast."

"Look, Jagger. Don't try to kid us, mate, with all your fancy chef's talk because we both know that this time last year the only meat you had was square sausage or corn beef."

"You can't beat a bit of corn beef. It's what we are made of. That and homemade lentil soup."

"Yeah, but these days it's more Pot Noodles and a few slices of bread."

Ringo asked the boys, "If you could only have one meal every day for the rest of your life what would it be?"

Jagger said, "That's easy. Curry, chicken curry. I would never get sick of that."

"Your ass would. What about you, Syd?"

"Well, I'm thinking toast and beans."

"Fuck off," said Ringo.

"What's up with toast and beans? It's good for you and it's like most of the birds you go with Ringo."

"I don't get it."

"Quick and easy."

"Funny cunt Syd."

"Well, what about you Ringo? I can't wait to hear this."

Ringo thought for a second then said, "Meringue."

The boys burst out laughing.

"Fucking meringue? No way."

"What's up with that? I have a sweet tooth."

"You wouldn't have a tooth left if you had meringue every day, ya daft cunt."

"Well, fuck yous two. I like meringue and I'm sticking with it. Anyway it's better than having curry or fucking beans every day, pair of smelly cunts. A lot of people like meringue."

"Well, I will say one thing, Ringo. Two meringues don't make a right."

Syd put his hand up. "Lads, can we stop talking about food for fuck's sake. I'm feeling sick here."

Jagger agreed. "Yeah, time for another wee line and a round, boys."

Later on as the night came to an end, Jagger went to get Sally from the lounge and she told him she would wait and get a taxi with Daisy so he should just walk home with Syd and Ringo.

He told her the good news that Ringo was staying at theirs for the night.

She said one word. "Smashing."

The boys all met at the pub door to smoke a joint which they did every time they left the pub.

"Full moon tonight, lads. Perfect night for a wee joint before bed."

Ringo took a puff then said, "Right, lads. No more lines tonight for me. I need to be up early and go into the toon get my wee brother the new Oasis CD. He has been asking for it all week, wee pain in the ass. Any of yous wanting to come with me?"

"No, thanks."

"We could get a few beers in town?"

"Ringo, mate, we can get a few beers here without going away into the toon. It's a shithole."

Syd took a big puff then said, "Right, lads. Stay safe. I'm away to get the heating on before Daisy gets in. Get the bed warm too."

"Easy, tiger," said Ringo.

Jagger and Ringo headed into the night.

CHAPTER 2

DON'T BE A PARTY POOPER...

Jagger stayed about a mile away from the pub but with Ringo in his ear it felt like ten miles.

"Where will I sleep, Jagger?"

"No' in with us, mate."

"I know that. It's just I don't want to be kipping on the floor. It fucks my back."

"You can sleep on the sofa. Don't worry."

"You got an extra pillow and blanket?"

"I should have a blanket but no' sure about a pillow."

"How do you not know if you have an extra pillow or not?"

"Because, Ringo, extra pillows is women's stuff I take fuck all to do with."

"I get that, mate, but you really should have an extra pillow for guests."

"We don't get many guests, mate."

"Well, you should still have an extra pillow for when your pal stays."

"And how the fuck was I to know you were staying? I have hairy balls, no' crystal balls."

As the boys headed towards the close that Jagger lived in they saw someone moving about at the back of his close but were not sure how many people there were because it was dark with the close lights not working.

"Who the fuck is that, Jagger? Do you know them?"

"No' sure who it is, but they can fuck off out my close, mate."

As they walked into the tenement they saw it looked like a couple kissing.

The guy turned round. "All right, lads. What's happening?"

"Fuck all but time to hit the road, love birds," said Jagger with Ringo standing behind him.

The guy walked into the light. It was the Crow and for once in his life he was trying to be nice. "All right, Jagger. I forgot you stayed here."

Jagger kept looking to see who was with him. "What's happening, mate? Why yous hiding in my close? You no' got a home or a bird to go to?"

"All right, Jagger. Don't get wide, mate."

Just as the Crow was talking a young girl walked into the light. It was Jagger's downstairs neighbour young Leeann and she was young too young to be in the dark with the Crow.

Jagger tried to keep his cool. He knew the last thing he needed was to fuck with the Crow. He wouldn't win so he took a second and a deep breath. "What yous up to, guys? Playing fucking hide and go seek?"

"No," said the Crow, "We were just having a wee cigarette and a chat, that's all. Ain't that right, Leeann?"

"Yes," she said with her eyes looking at the ground.

"Well, it's getting late. Time to call it a night."

"You telling me what to do, Jagger?"

"Sounds like it, aye."

"Easy, mate," whispered Ringo.

"Well, maybe you're right, Jagger. It is getting late and maybe I will see you tomorrow for a wee chat."

Ringo told the Crow, "No, mate. It's all good here. No need for a chat. We know the score."

"I know you fucking do, Ringo. I just hope your mate does too."

The Crow walked away into the night leaving just Jagger, Ringo and young Leeann.

"You head up the stair, Ringo. I will be up in a minute."

"Ok, mate. I will get the kettle on and roll one."

Jagger talked to Leeann. "You ok, pal?"

"Yeah, I'm fine."

"Did he hurt you?"

"No. What you talking about, hurt me? He likes me."

"You could do a lot better than that fucker. He is bad news and too old for you."

"Leave it, Jagger. You're no' my da. Fuck, I don't even know who my da is. That's how fucked up my life is."

"It won't get any better with him in it. Trust me."

"Look, Jagger. I know you and Sally always look out for me but I'm seventeen. I can do what I want."

"I'm sorry, pal. I don't want to upset you. Do you want me to get sally to pop in and see you?"

"Maybe tomorrow."

Jagger walked away.

Leeann got to her door and before she walked in she said, "Goodnight, Jagger, and thanks."

"No bother, pal. Goodnight."

Jagger headed up the stairs into his flat. Ringo was sitting rolling a joint.

"You get the kettle on, Ringo?"

"No, mate. No' yet. I was thinking it was maybe best to get a wee number rolled first."

"Cool. I will get it. What do you take with your tea again?"

"Two rolls and square sausage, thanks."

"You know what I mean, funny cunt."

"Just two sugars, mate. No milk for me. That's no' right. Cunts drinking milk."

Jagger walked back into the room. "I'm going to regret this but what's up with milk?"

"What's right with it you should maybe be asking? Fucking drinking milk from an animal? No way, mate. That will fuck up your insides."

"Yeah because all the drink and drugs won't, but milk will. Very good, Ringo."

As Jagger came back in with the tea Ringo asked him, "Well, would you drink your mum's milk?"

"Hold the bus. Don't be bringing my ma's tits into this or you will be sleeping in the close."

"I'm no' talking about your ma's tits. I'm talking about drinking milk from a human. It's no' right, is it?"

"No, it's no'. It's fucked up but I don't want to talk. I just want a cup of tea and a joint to help me come coon off the coke and the drink, ok?"

"Yeah, fine, mate. Sounds good. Any blues?"

"Yeah, I will get us a few before bed."

"Yass, mate. A wee hill street blues will help chase the demons away."

"You're only getting one. I'm no' having you walking about my flat out your nut on Valium."

"I know you don't want to talk but we need to talk about what just happened tonight with the Crow."

"Fuck him. I said what had to be said. It's done now as long as he stays away from wee Leeann."

"Look. You don't fuck with the Crow. He is a sneaky cunt and he won't think twice about stabbing you."

"I know, mate, but I can't just stand back and watch him mess about with that wee lassie. He will destroy his life."

"I know that but if you get in his way, he will destroy you and me."

"How will he destroy you?"

"Because if he sets about you, I will fucking set about him. I know the meaning of the word pals. If he sets about you, I will fucking kill the cunt."

"That's the drink talking. Chill out, mate, and smoke the joint. We will worry about it another day, mate."

"Cool. Jagger, can I tell you something?"

"Sure, what is it?"

"Your tea is rotten, mate."

"How the fuck can it be rotten? It's only hot water and a fucking tea bag. How can anyone fuck that up?"

"I don't know but you did."

"Fuck off. Any cunt can make a cup of tea without milk or sugar. Even Del the Smell couldn't fuck that up and he is a fucking idiot."

"He is, isn't he?" laughed Ringo. "Do you know when we were wee guys he called his granny 'Mum' and told us his mum was his sister. Now that's fucked up."

"Yeah, I remember but that happened a lot and always because the mum was so young when she had the kid the family tried to hide it from the neighbours."

"I know but then the kid gets all fucking messed up because as he gets older he is no' sure if his cousin is his fucking uncle."

"Yep, fucking Glasgow hillbillies."

Ringo randomly hit out with, "I fucked an American once."

"What the fuck has that got to do with anything, mate?"

"You were talking about hillbillies and they are American and it made me think of her. She was lovely. Her name was Pamela. She was from Toronto."

"Toronto is in Canada, mate."

"Well, same thing. She was over for the school summer holiday and I fucked her round the back of my gran's close."

"Every boy in Glasgow has made out to have shagged a bird round at their granny's bit."

"Well, I did, so if you don't believe me then fucking tough. Have you shagged an American?"

"Yeah, when I went on holiday to Florida I met this hot black girl."

"Was she a hooker?"

"No, was she fuck. She worked in the bar I went into. We had a few drinks then went back to my hotel."

"What was her name?"

"Honey."

"Yeah, she was a hooker, mate."

"Why? Because of her name?"

"Yeah. Didn't it bother you that her name was a cool as fuck hooker name?"

"No, I didn't care. I knew that was probably no' her name but I wasn't giving a fuck. I had other things on my mind and it's no' as if I was wanting her real name. I wasn't looking for a pen pal."

"Did yous go for it all night?"

"I wish, mate. I was too fucking drunk. All I remember was her about to take her clothes off when she asked me, 'Have you ever seen an American woman naked?' I said, 'Only in the movies, hen,' then we went for it."

"Did you keep in touch?"

"No. When I woke in the morning, she was gone but then at lunchtime she phoned the room I was in and asked if I would like to take her for brunch."

"What's that?"

"Breakfast slash lunch but I said no."

"And what did she say?"

"It's funny, mate. I will never forget what she said to me for the rest of my life."

"Well, what the fuck was it?"

"She said, 'Come on, Jagger. Don't be a party pooper.'"

"Fuck off." Ringo burst out laughing.

"Come to think about it now. She was a hooker. Fucking honey."

"Hey, mate, if I ever go to Florida I hope I bump into her."

"Just you worry about making it to Benidorm, mate. Now let's get you a wee blue and get to sleep. If Sally comes in and finds us talking about hookers, she will be doing more moaning than a French hooker."

Meanwhile Syd was having a better night then his pals. He went back with Daisy to her mum and dad's house hoping to get his end away. Syd and Daisy had only been going out with each other a few months but Syd was head over heels in love with her and just as well, Daisy was feeling the same about Syd.

The only problem was Syd stayed with his brother who only had a one-bedroom flat so they could never get much alone time and it was driving them crazy. They just wanted their own wee flat to hideaway from everyone and be together and shag. But Daisy was only eighteen but was working two jobs trying to save for a deposit for a wee flat but Syd was spending more than he was making so for now they were going nowhere.

The only time they got together was a few hours in Jagger and Sally's flat when they were at work or like tonight Syd could come and sit in Daisy's room for an hour but not any longer than an hour or her mum and dad would think they were up to no good.

As they headed into Daisy's house they were greeted by her wee dog Turbo. He was going nuts to see them both.

"Where is my boy?" Daisy picked him up and walked into the front room to see her mum and dad.

"Hi, guys," her mum said, "How was your shift, hen?"

"It was busy, Mum. What yous up to?"

"Nothing much. Just having a wee drink and watching the telly. How you doing, Syd?"

"I'm good, thanks."

"You working yet?"

"I'm no' working yet, no, but have a few things lined up you know."

"Mum, me and Syd are just going to sit and play some music before he heads home."

"Yeah, hen. Just keep it down a bit."

"We will, Mum."

"He is no' staying long," her dad said without even looking at them.

"We know, Dad. We are just having a cup of tea then he will be away."

They ran into the room and shut the door.

"Get some music, quick," Syd said taking his gear off.

"What do you want on, Syd?"

"I'm no' giving a fuck. I want you on that bed so I can get into your fine China so hurry up."

After Syd gave Daisy five minutes of hard shagging, she got ready and went to put the kettle on so it looked like they were not up to anything. As Syd put his gear back on, he sat back on the bed and lit a cigarette. As he was sitting, chilling and having his smoke, wee turbo came in sniffing about. He headed over to the bin at the side of the bed and stuck his wee nose in.

"What you up to, Turbo? There is no food in there, son."

Turbo brought his wee head out the bin with a condom in his wee gob.

Syd took a closer look. "What the fuck? No, Turbo, give it here."

Turbo took a step back.

"Good boy, yaw wee shithead, give that here."

Then in that second Syd found out why they called him Turbo. He was off out the room. Syd couldn't do nothing, only sit on the bed praying he took it into Daisy and not the front room.

Within two seconds he heard her dad shout, "What the fuck is that the dog's got?"

Syd just sat with his heads in his hands.

Daisy ran into the front room. "What's up, Dad?" Then Syd heard Daisy too, saying, "Oh my fucking God."

The front room was chaos. They were all running about going nuts. The only cunt enjoying itself was wee Turbo. As they chased after him, he spilt spunk all over the front room carpet. Syd tried to explain but they were having none of it.

Daisy told him to go.

The next morning Ringo was up and out early. It was 9:35 a.m. and that was early for Ringo who woke up most days to the sound of *Home and Away* playing on the TV. He was sitting at the bus stop cold and hungover and the sun wasn't even up yet. As he sat having a smoke, looking up the road for the bus, an old lady sat down beside him. "Morning, hen, you ok?"

"Yes, son, I'm good."

"You going into the toon for a bit of shopping?"

"No, I'm going down to the hospital."

"Hope you're ok."

"I'm fine, son. Thanks."

As Ringo put out his smoke, she asked him, "hat you up to today?"

"I'm going to the toon to pick up my wee brother a CD."

"That's nice. You sound like a good brother."

"Yeah, some cun—I mean, someone has to look out for him."

"I hope the sun comes out like yesterday. It's too cold this morning."

"Yeah, I'm sure it will. Maybe just in time for me to get a wee pint in the town after my shopping is done."

"Hope so, son."

As Ringo moved a bit on the bus stop where him and the old dear were sitting, he felt his right bum cheek was a bit

30

uncomfortable. He put his hand down to rub his cheek and it was all wet. "What the fuck? I think this seat is all wet, hen. Watch where you're sitting."

The old dear looked at the seat and then looked in her bag. "Oh no, it's my sample for the hospital. It's leaking."

"What the fucking hell? Please tell me that's no' piss, hen."

"Yes, the doctor told me to bring a sample with me. I must of no' tightened the lid right."

Ringo tried to keep his cool but inside he was going nuts. "I'm so sorry."

"It's ok, hen. These things happen."

"Here, get yourself a pint." She handed him a twenty-pound note.

"No, you're ok, but thanks anyway."

"No, I feel bad. Here, take it and get a wee beer on me."

Ringo took it, looking around making sure no cunt was watching.

Half an hour later Ringo was in HMV. He grabbed the Oasis CD then headed over to the Beatles albums. He already had them all but any fan will tell you when you're in a record shop you need to have a look at your favourite band. Just like Jagger would with the Rolling Stones or Syd with the Sex Pistols.

As Ringo was looking through the albums, a lady softly put her hand on his shoulder. "Son?" she said.

Ringo turned round to look at her. "Hi. You ok, hen?"

"I'm sorry. For a second there I thought you were my son."

"That's ok. It happens. Is he kicking about in here?"

"No, he passed away in a car crash last year and now I keep thinking I see him. I'm a daft old cow."

"No you're no'. You're just a mum who is missing her son. I understand it. Must be hell."

"You looking at the Beatles albums?"

"Yeah, I love the Beatles. My favourite band. I love them that much my pals call me Ringo."

"That's a cool nickname."

"My mate, we call him Jagger."

"Let me guess. He is a Rolling Stones' fan."

"He keeps telling me that the Stones are a better band than the Beatles but I tell him the Beatles are the best band in the world and no cunt will ever be better than the Beatles."

"My boy loved the Beatles too. I play them all the time and it helps."

"Yeah, the Beatles have got me through some hard times, hen."

"It's been lovely talking to you. I will let you get on with your shopping."

"It was nice to meet you, hen."

"It really is mad how much you look like him."

"He must have been a good looking boy then."

"See, as I am leaving the shop would it be ok if I said to you, 'Bye, son, see you later,' or would that be weird?"

"No, that's fine. If it makes you feel better then I'm good with it."

"Thanks and have a nice day, Ringo."

A few moments later, as Ringo was still looking at all the Beatles albums he already has, he heard the women at the till say, "Bye, son. I will see you later."

He looked round and saw her wee sad face standing at the checkout.

"Ok, bye," he said to hopefully make her feel better.

The women smiled for a second and walked out the door. Ringo thought, *What a fucking day and I have no' even had a beer yet.* He took the Oasis CD up to the checkout.

The guy scanned it and said, "Will that be all, mate?"

"Yeah, thanks, mate."

"Ninety-five pounds please."

"Ninety-five pounds for a fucking CD?"

"No. That and all the albums your mum got too."

"What you talking about, mate?"

"Your mum was just here. She said you were getting her stuff. You were just picking one more CD but she was in a hurry."

"That was no' my fucking mum."

"Yeah, well, when she said, 'Bye, son,' why did you say bye back then?"

"Fucking dirty sneaky low life cow told me some bullshit story about how I looked like her dead son."

"Look, mate if you're no' paying then I need to get the cops to yous."

"What the fuck have I done? I done fuck all."

"You might be in on it."

"Look, mate. I have a fucking banging hangover and I don't need this shit today so keep your fucking CD. I will get it cheaper in Virgin anyway."

Ringo threw the CD down and walked fast out the shop and ran down the side street heading for the bus home.

Jagger and Syd were already in the pub when Ringo walked in from his eventful day out in the town.

"All right, boys. You want a beer? I'm buying. It's been a cunt of a day."

"Ringo, we would love a wee beer. Thanks."

As Ringo sat down, Jagger looked at him and Syd and said, "Cheer up, boys, it might never happen."

"It already ready has, mate. I was on my way into the toon to get that CD and I sat on piss at the bus stop. I had to go home and change before I came here."

"Thank fuck you did," said Syd.

"And then some bird gave me a bullshit story about her son being dead, trying to get me to pay for her stuff. The cunt in the shop was wanting to jail me. I had to get off. It was a nightmare, boys. I'm telling you. I hate the fucking toon. That's why I try and avoid it."

"Well, it sounds like you had a cunt of a day, Ringo. And poor Syd had a cunt of a night."

"Why? What happened last night?"

"Well, after me and Daisy had sex, her wee dog Turbo grabbed the condom out the bin and ran into the front room with it in front of her ma and da."

The boys were laughing.

"It's no' fucking funny, lads. Her ma and da are going nuts."

Jagger said, "Well, mate, at least they know she is having safe sex."

"No, lads. It's bad. We hardly have anywhere to go by ourselves as it is and now this happens. I feel I have more bad luck than a young guy on the Titanic celebrating his eighteenth birthday."

Jagger told him, "Look, don't worry too much about it. They will forget about it before you know it and it will be the funny story they tell at Christmas. Trust me, mate."

Ringo randomly added, "I hate condoms."

"Ok, Ringo, we will bite. Tell us why you hate them. Maybe give us a laugh."

"I hate everything about them. From being embarrassed to buying to the feeling you get with them on. It's like having a bath with your socks on."

"We hear you, mate, but they do stop the spread of HIV and unwanted pregnancy."

"I know all that. It's just I'm no' into them and you know what I hate the most about them?"

"No, what?"

"Well, you know when you're shagging a bird and you're done."

"What, after two minutes?"

"No. When you have been in bed giving her it good style. It's been all nice and you feel like you have satisfied her and you sit at the end of the bed asking how was it for her. And she is all happy and wanting a smoke and then you whip off the condom and you start to unroll the rest of the condom you didn't need and it just keeps going unrolling and you're thinking, *Whose cock is this made for fucking King Kong?*"

"Well, Ringo. I'm with Syd on wearing a condom. As my old granny always told me: no balloons, no party, son."

"Wise women your granny."

"Hell yes."

"I know it's the done thing so you don't catch anything and that."

"More chance some poor wee bird gets something from you, Ringo."

"What the fuck do you mean?"

"Well, all the birds you have been with… none of them were virgins, mate. They had all been round the block. And all were ruff as fuck, mate."

"No' all of them. Yous are making out all I do is fuck dirty cows."

"Well, Ringo, you only need to shag one sheep to be a sheep shagger."

"Not all of them were cows. What about wee Linda Johnson from your work? I took her out. She was a nice lassie."

"She was, mate, but she wasn't a looker now, was she?"

"What do you mean?"

"What I mean, Ringo, and I will say this in a nice way, is I wouldn't ride her into battle."

"That's sick, lads. Talking about a girl like that. Now one of yous cunts hit the bar before I hit yous."

As Syd came back with the beers Ringo asked him, "Did Jagger tell that his night was just as bad as our night?"

"No, what happened?"

"Nothing happened."

Syd looked at Ringo. "You tell then, Ringo."

"He had a run in with the Crow."

"No way. How and where?"

"Outside my close. He was sniffing about my young neighbour wee Leeann."

"And Jagger had a go at him for it and the Crow wasn't happy but he let it go and left."

"Maybe you should let it go, Jagger. You don't want to be fucking about with him. He is nuts."

"I'm no' fucking going ahead with him or anything."

"Good because he would stab you to death, mate."

"Syd is right. No cunts will mess with him because if you beat him in a fist fight he will just come back for you with a knife. The guy doesn't give a fuck about the jail. Unlike guys like us, he can do hard time like a walk in the park."

"I could do time as well."

"No' hard time and you're too pretty for the jail, Jagger. They would be selling your wee skinny ass for a packet of tobacco, mate."

"Ringo is right. No cunt will dig him. Even Cagney and Lacey don't dig him up for dealing in here. Rhey know he would wreck the pub if they did."

"Yous know why he is so fucking mental?"

"No, why?"

"Because of what happened to his family?"

"No, Ringo, we don't know but need to now."

"Well, the Crow had a happy childhood at first. Him, his big brother and his mum and dad. His dad worked in the shop yards but he always spent his weekends with his two boys taking them to the game and all that. Then one night his big brother, who was about fifteen at the time, was walking home from his weeknight boys' club when three guys all aged about eighteen or nineteen stopped him down the lane from were Syd stays now. They dug him asking where he was from and did he have any money. His brother was scared and made a run for it but the three guys went after him and when they got him one of them stabbed him in the back of his leg saying to him, 'You can't run now, wee man.' Then they all walked away laughing."

"Did he die?"

"Yeah, a few feet from his house. The Crow and his pal found him. The pal said the blood was everywhere. Poor cunt. They hit his main artery and left him to die alone in the cold dark street."

"So that's why the Crow is a fucking mental case"

"No, that's just half the story, lads. They got the guy who done it and he went down for it. He got like ten years but the Crow's dad was never the same. He stopped going to work and was always drinking."

"Well, you can't blame the guy for that. The poor cunt lost his son."

"Yeah, but after like six years, the guy got out. You know, for like good behaviour. And then the Crow's da changed. He gave up the drink and was out walking and going to the gym. It was weird. It was if he was happy the lad was out."

"Was he getting himself in shape to set about the guy?"

"Yep, that's the way it was looking, but the guy was sorry for what he did and told people he was young and daft. He was just wanting to move on from it all. And so he did he got a job and met a bird and before long they moved in together and within a year or two they had a kid too. But what no one knew, especially the guy, was that the Crow's da had been watching him everywhere he went. The pub or work, a day out with the lads… he was always standings in the shadows and all that time he had nothing to do with his other son, the Crow.

"Every time he would ask his dad to play football or take him to the park, his da would tell him he was too busy. And he was. He was busy watching this cunt's every move just waiting to get him. This went on for like five years then one sunny Saturday afternoon the guy took his wife and wee two-and-a-bit son on the Waverley for a day out down the Clyde. They were standing on the deck no' knowing that the Crow's da was on board watching him.

"The guy went to get his family some ice cream and as they handed him the three ice creams he handed one to his wife then when he was just about to ask his wife where their boy was, they heard his scream. They looked over to find the Crow's da holding the wee boy over the side. They ran over begging not to let him go. The Crow's da asked him, 'Do you know who I am?' The guy said, 'I think so.' He said, 'You killed my son for nothing.' 'I'm so sorry,' the guy said. 'He was a good boy, my son, and you fucking killed him to act the big man.' 'I'm so sorry.' 'You're no' even close to sorry but now you can live with the pain like I did,' and he let the wee boy go into the Clyde."

"Fucking hell. You're joking…" said Jagger.

"No. The guy jumped in after his wee boy and the mother was hitting the Crow's da but he didn't move or say another word. When the cops got him, he went without a fight into the police car. The guy apparently almost drowned trying to get to his wee boy but witnesses later said in court they seen the Crow's da putting a weight down the wee boy's trousers before he picked the wee soul up."

"That's fucked up, Ringo."

"I know but it's true. So after all that, the Crow's wee ma hit the drink big time. She couldn't stand everyone pointing the finger at her as if she had done it. She didn't last long after it anyway so the Crow didn't just lose his big brother. He lost his mum and dad too. He went from home to home then in and out the jail. And that's why the Crow is the mad crazy cunt we know now."

CHAPTER 3

FUN IN THE SUN...

A few nights before the boys planned to go away on holiday Ringo was sitting in a strange pub. He had never been in this pub before in his life. It was quite quiet for it was a school night. Not many cunts out for a drink on the week days. This was just what Ringo wanted. As he sat alone having his beer he tried his best to keep himself to himself as Ringo was up to no good.

He sat looking about, trying to play it cool, holding onto a black Puma spots bag. He was holding onto it like it had a thousand pounds in it. But it didn't. What it had in it was his da's old sawed off shotgun that Ringo had taken without his old man knowing. In fact his old dad thought that no cunt knew he had a gun. Especially Ringo because he knew his son Ringo was a dirty sticky fingers wee cunt. But Ringo knew were everything was in their house from his dad's gun or porno stash to his mum's old vibrator that was kept in a box in her room drawer beside her Valium that Ringo liked to help himself to when he had the fear from the drink.

Ringo took the last sip of his pint and headed out the door into the night. He was not here to rob the pub. Too many cunts in it. No, he was going to rob the Chinese takeaway shop next door that was down a dark lane out the way.

Ringo stood outside the Ruby Panda waiting for the shop to be empty. As the last customer left Ringo walked in.

"What you want? We are about to close."

Ringo slapped the shotgun on the counter. "I want your money, sweetheart."

"You no funny. You put that away or I will tell the police."

"Listen. You empty that fucking till or I will empty this shooter. Now fucking move."

The wee women started to empty the till into the bag. "You wee bad boy, you fucking prick. I hope the police get you and put you in cell."

"I'm sure they will some day, hen."

Just then the Chinese chef came running out from the back with a meat cleaver.

Ringo swung the gun in his direction. "Hold your horses, mate. You come any closer and I will spread your nut all over that menu behind you."

The chef came a bit closer.

"I'm fucking warning you, Ping Pong. You're fucking getting it."

"No, you stop. Take the money now. Go, leave."

Ringo ran out the door and into the night. He headed down the lane then over a fence running through all the back gardens to keep off the street and out of the way. Ringo got home covered in sweat and mud and he headed right into his room to see much he had, but his wee brother walked in.

"Fuck off out my room."

"What you up to?"

"Fuck all."

"Why you out of breath? You been fighting?"

"No, now piss off, mate."

"You better tell me or I'm telling Mum you're all muddy and out of breath."

Ringo stuck his hand in the bag, pulled out a five-pound note and handed it to his wee brother. "Here take this and piss off. And don't be telling Ma or Da, ok?"

His wee brother took the note so fast it burnt Ringo's fingers.

Ringo locked the bedroom door and poured the money onto his bed. He opened a can of beer and started to count all the notes and all the coins with a big smile on his face, happy that he now had his spending money for his holiday.

The next day Ringo was up early. He couldn't sleep with his body still buzzing with adrenaline. He made his way up to see Jagger to give him the money as he was the one taking everyone's spending money to the post office to change it into pesetas.

"Morning, mate."

"Morning, Ringo. Come in. You're up early."

"I know, mate. I couldn't fucking sleep."

"Sally is making breakfast. You wanting some?"

"No, mate. I'm no' hungry, thanks. I just want to give you my spending money for the post office."

Ringo handed Jagger the bag full of notes and coins.

"What the fuck is this, Ringo?"

"What? It's my money."

"What did you do, rob your wee brother's piggy bank? What the fuck have I to do with coins?"

"What you're going to do is take them to the post office."

Sally walked in. "Morning, Ringo."

"Morning, hen."

She looked in the bag. "Fucking hell, Ringo. You rob a bank?"

"No, I didn't, ok?"

Jagger just stood there looking at him. "Where the fuck did you get this, mate?"

"I got it selling hash. What's the big deal?"

"I will tell you what the big deal is, mate. You don't take ten- and twenty-pence coins off of cunts who are buying hash off you. That's the big deal."

"Well, the coins I had in a jar in my room. I was saving for my holiday."

Sally said, "I can always tell when you're lying, Ringo."

"How?"

"Because your lips always move."

"Funny. Ha fucking ha, Sally. Right, I'm off. I will see yous later."

Jagger got Ringo to the door. They didn't say a word to each other and he walked back in to sit with Sally.

"Where do you think he got the money?" she asked.

"I don't know and I don't want to know. The only thing I'm worrying about is I need to take that cash into the post office and as soon as I hand it over the cops show up."

"Don't take it then. Let Ringo take it."

"I wish I could but Ringo is barred from the post office and anyway if he took it in the cops would fucking show up."

The next day a very pissed off Jagger walked into the post office. There was a big line full of old dears all waiting and talking, not one of them was in a hurry. Jagger stood there patiently waiting in line talking to himself.

"Fucking hurry up and stop talking shit."

The next woman got served.

"Hi, can I post this to my sister in Australia, hen?"

"First class or second?"

"I'm no' sure. Maybe second… No, make it first class, hen."

"Ok, what's in the parcel?"

"It's a video tape, hen, of my daughter's wedding."

"That's nice. Was it a lovely wedding? I bet she was beautiful."

"She was, so we got two videos done so I could send one to my sister Linda. She has been out there for years. It's a shame. She was so upset she couldn't make it."

Jagger was losing the will to live. He was talking to himself trying to keep his cool. "Hurry the fuck up. No cunt cares about your fat daughter's shit wedding."

"Right, next."

A wee old lady was next and she took about five minutes to get to the counter.

"Can I post this letter please?"

"Sure, my love, where is it going?"

"Paisley."

Jagger was screaming inside. Fucking Paisley? She could get a bus and save on the fucking stamp. He looked down the line and behind him, wishing they would all hurry up. Just as he was thinking it wasn't that bad he would be served soon, the door opened and a young mother tried to get in with her daughter in a buggy. Jagger helped her and she said thank you.

As Jagger said, "You're welcome," he noticed she was a pretty good looking mum. He gave her a smile and she gave him one back. Jagger looked at her wee girl in the buggy but he noticed that she is not that wee. In fact she was a bit big for a buggy then it clicked with him that she was handicapped. He looked away fast not wanting to be rude.

The wee girl in the buggy started shouting, "Mum, I need the toilet."

"Just wait a minute, Lucy. We won't be long in here."

Jagger turned and asked her, "Do you want to go in front of me?"

"No, but thanks anyway."

The wee girl kept going. "I need the toilet, Mum. I need the toilet."

"Just wait, Lucy. We won't be long."

"Mum, I just done a piss in my nappy."

Jagger was thinking, *Beam me up, Scotty, for fuck's sake.*

Next thing the wee girl grabbed Jagger's ass and shouted, "Hey, you. You're ugly."

Jagger was like, *No, God, why me?* He looked round. "Ok, now that's plenty, pal."

She grabbed his ass again. "Hey, you. You're ugly."

Her mum tried to get her into trouble. "Lucy, stop it right now."

"No, I can do what I want and I want to feel his bum."

Jagger turned back round. "If I'm ugly then why you wanting to feel my bum, pal?"

"Because I can do what I want."

The mum told her, "No, stop it," but it was no good. She kept going, "Ugly bum, ugly!"

Jagger couldn't take any more. He turned round and said, "I'm fucking ugly? I don't think so, pal. You're the ugly wee fucker in here. I mean, what age are you? Like fucking fourteen or something?

"She is only twelve," the shocked young mother told him.

"Ok, then a big twelve and still a buggy and a fucking nappy for fuck's sake, but I'm the ugly cunt? Aye, right."

"You need to leave, son," the woman behind the counter said.

"No, I need to get my peseta money then I will go."

"No, son, you will go now or I'm calling the police."

"Ok, fine then, but I'm no' the one in the wrong here."

All the old dears stood in the line shaking their heads at him.

Jagger headed to the next post office with his bag of cash. It was four miles away and it was pissing down with rain. By the time he got the pesetas and got back to the pub he was wet to the bone.

He walked into the nice warm and dry pub where Syd and Ringo were sitting enjoying a nice cold beer.

"All right, mate. Fucking hell, is it raining out there?"

"Wee bit, just a wee bit."

"You're fucking ringing, mate."

"I know, thanks."

"You're ringing more than my ma's phone when my auntie Jean has a bit of gossip, mate."

"I won't sit as I'm no' staying. Just popped in to make sure you got the gear."

"We got it, mate. Did you get the pesetas?"

"Yeah, I did. Now I'm going home to spend time with my bird and get a warm and early night I think. Yous two should do the same."

"I would love an early night with Sally," said Ringo.

"You know what I mean. And on your way to mine tomorrow don't forget the condoms for the gear."

"Can you no' pick them up on your way home?"

"No, I fucking can't, mate. How do you think I will look picking up condoms and Sally sees them and I'm away on holiday tomorrow?"

"Just tell her they're for putting the gear up our ass."

"Just you get them, Ringo, on your way home."

"Me and Syd are staying here a bit longer."

"Well, don't be staying out getting drunk."

Syd said, "No, mate. Ringo has his eye on a wee bird over there and he wants me to help him talk to her pal."

"If Daisy walks in and sees you, she will kill you."

"She's already no' talking to me with the hard time from her family over that fucking condom, mate."

"What bird you eyeing up, Ringo?"

"Her over there with the black hair."

"Her with the big ass?"

"Yeah, that's her. She is going to get into so much trouble tonight and she doesn't even know it yet."

"She is no' much of a looker, is she?"

"She's all right. You saying she's ugly?"

"I'm no' saying she's an ugly cunt but she should have her own flavour of Monster Munch, mate."

The next morning a very hungover Ringo and Syd showed up at Jagger's door.

"Morning, lads. How's things? You want a wee bit of eggs and a few greasy sausages?"

"Fuck up, Jagger and get us a beer."

The boys stood in Jagger's small kitchen having a beer looking at what was on the table. Jagger went over everything with them.

"Right, ladies, what we have here is a jar of Vaseline, a packet of condoms and a no' bad bag of coke spilt into three and a wee bag of pills."

"I'm no' happy about putting this up my arse."

"Well, Syd, unless you can think of another way we will be happy to hear your ideas."

"I'm just saying it no' right. My hole is exit only, lads."

"Why don't you bring Daisy's wee dog? He's good at handling condoms."

"Aye, wee fucking Turbo could take it all and run past security with it."

"You're no' fucking funny, boys. I'm away to sit and have a beer and think of another way." Syd took another beer, his share of the coke and walked out the kitchen.

"Right, Ringo. You can go first. Grease the condom up and stick it up your back door."

Ringo walked into the toilet and was back out within two minutes.

"Fucking hell, Ringo, you done it already?"

"No' the first time I've had to stick something up my prison pocket, mate. You forget I was in the jail."

Jagger went in next, struggling to get the job done.

"How you getting on, Jagger?" Ringo asked through the door.

"I'm trying here, mate."

"What's taking so long? The taxi will be here soon."

"I know and you talking to me is no' helping any."

"Look, you're sticking a condom up your arse no' making love, so hurry up."

"It feels like King Kong's thumb instead of mine."

A few moments later Jagger came out the toilet.

"Fucking hell, mate. You're all sweaty. Did you have an orgasm?"

"I don't want to talk about."

"Yeah, all right, Rod Stewart. Let's see how Syd is doing with his."

They found Syd sitting having his beer with a smile on his face.

"You having sex with yourself too?"

"No. I worked out a better way to take my coke on holiday."

"Ok, tell us."

"Well, we're taking Askit powders with us so I just put it in the wee Askit packets."

"We need the Askits for our hangovers."

"I will pick up more on the way."

"Cool. Just don't mix them up. I don't need that first thing in the morning with a fucking hangover."

The boys got to the airport and checked in, heading right up to security to get it out the way. As they stood in the line Jagger laughed saying, "Right, everybody, be cool. Ringo, you be cool."

Ringo liked the joke but Syd wasn't taking it in.

"You ok, Syd?"

"No. Maybe I should've stuck it up my arse. I mean what if they look into the Askit box?"

"It's ok, mate. Chill out."

"Yeah, I'm good. Talk about something to keep my mind off it."

Ringo asked Jagger, "Did you put in holidays or phone in sick for work?"

"I phoned in, mate. Said I have the flu."

"Who the fuck gets the flu in the summer."

"Lots of people, mate."

"Well, it's better than last year when you coloured in your toe with a black maker saying you broke it."

"Yeah, the doctor had fucking ink on his fingers. He was looking at his own pen as I walked out with my sick line."

As they stood laughing, the big security guy shouted, "Next!"

"Right, Syd, move," said Ringo.

Syd walked up shaking like mad with his head looking down at the floor.

Ringo said, "This is bad. He's going to fuck this up."

Jagger said, "Fucking hell, he's standing there like Elvis, all shook up."

The big guard looked at Syd. "You ok, sir?"

"Who, me? Yeah, I'm fine. Wee bit of a hangover and that."

"You got anything on you I should know about?"

"Me? No way, no, mate. I mean sir."

"Are you carrying a large amount of money with you today that we should know about?"

"Well, yeah, sir, maybe."

"You are? How much?"

"Well, my mum gave me sixty pounds. You know, for like emergencies and you know..."

"Well, I'm sure I can let you go with that amount. On your way."

The boys ran to the bar to get their holiday started. Syd hit the bar feeling a lot better now he was safe from getting a finger up his back door. Jagger and Ringo went to find a table in the busy airport bar.

"Let's get a table here, Jagger, by the window."

"Yeah, cool, mate. This will do."

"Look, Jagger. That guy behind you has just dropped his wallet."

"Here, mate. Did you drop this?" Jagger handed the guy his wallet with all his holiday money in it. "You would have been fucked if my pal didn't notice it."

The guy took his wallet and looked away without saying anything.

"Fuck's his problem?"

"I don't know. Maybe he is just a wanker."

"No, mate. It's the place that dose it."

"Does what, mate?"

"Two things in life that turn people into wankers: airports and Christmas."

"You might be on to something there, mate."

As the boys sat drinking many pints, they watched everyone going by running to their gate. As they were getting another round in, a group of girls walked in.

"Here we go, lads. Bellies in, the birds are here," Ringo said.

Jagger came back with the drinks. "I knew that would cheer you up, Ringo."

"It does, mate, and now we play the airport game."

"What's that?"

"Well, we all pick a good looking bird and bet ten pounds each which one of them will be staying at our hotel."

"Sounds like a shit game."

"And if the one you like is at your hotel I know how to get talking to her."

"Go on."

"Well, when you see her the first day at the pool what do you check out first?"

"Her tits and ass."

"No, her beach towel."

"Why her fucking towel?"

"Because the next day you get up early and you put your towel beside her towel then you have all day to talk and have a drink with her and her pals."

"You know, Ringo, you are a genius."

"Or he is just a pervert."

As Syd sipped his beer he went white and had the same look as he did in the security line.

"You ok, Syd?"

"No. The cops are over there and they have a fucking sniffer dog."

"It's ok. As long as it doesn't sniff our ass we will be fine."

"One problem there… dogs like to sniff ass."

"Fuck up, Ringo, and go and get Syd a Valium out of your prison pocket."

"That's going to be a nightmare taking it out to put it back in."

"Well, he needs to chill out so move."

Ringo headed into the airport toilets. He looked around for an empty cubicle and finally found one. He went in and started to push out his bag. Just as he was pushing he heard a guy banging on the doors. He had a panic in his voice.

"Any of these empty? I need to go real bad." He banged on the cubicle that Ringo was in.

"There is someone in here."

"You going to be long, mate? I need a shit real bad like."

"Well, I'm in the middle of a Star Trek shit, mate."

"Star Trek? What's that?"

"It means I'm having trouble with the cling-ons. Now piss off."

An hour or so later a very chilled out Syd was sitting enjoying his beer. As he looked around at the police walking by or the dogs sniffing about he didn't care one bit. The blues and the beers had kicked in.

Ringo went to the bar and to talk to the girls on his way to the bar.

Jagger asked, "Syd, you ok now, mate?"

"Yes, I'm fine, mate. I'm just watching the world go by."

"Good, mate. Won't be long and we will be in the sun."

"You know, it's a wee shame."

"What is?"

"The dogs in here. It's no' right."

"What you talking about, Syd?"

"Well, the sniffer dogs, they have a job. You don't see many dogs with jobs anymore."

"You don't see many cunts in Glasgow with jobs either."

"Yeah, that's right, Jagger, but it must be shit for the cop dogs having to work. I mean, imagine you were a wee sniffer dog and it's a sunny day outside and all the other dogs in your street are over at the park playing catch and you can't go because you're night shift. That's fucking sad, mate."

"Don't worry, Syd. I'm sure they get double time for it."

Ringo walked up to the girls at the other table. "All right, ladies. I need to ask you something. Do you like football?"

"No."

"Do you like chess then?"

"No."

"Well, do you like golf then?"

"No!"

"Well, good. I will sit here then because that's all my pals are talking about. So, where we off to?"

"Benidorm."

"Same here."

"Is your pal over there ok? He looks no' well."

"Who, Syd? No, he is fine. He was just having a wee panic attack because we have cocaine up our back doors and he thinks the wee sniffer dog might sniff our ass."

"Well, that's lovely but we need to get to our gate. It was nice talking to you."

"And you, sweetheart. Maybe we will be in the same hotel."

"Hope no'."

"What did you say?"

"I said hope so."

As the girls walked way Ringo shouted, "Bye, girls. Can't wait to see your white bits at the pool."

CHAPTER 4

DRUGS, PUBS AND NIGHT CLUBS...

The boys got to the hotel after a long hot bus ride from the airport. Jagger went to the wee shop beside the hotel to get the beers for the room and Ringo and Syd went and checked in.

As they headed into their new home for the next few days, Ringo fell onto the bed and Syd went to check out the view. As he stood there looking at the blue sea and the golden beach, he thought about how beautiful it was and how it would be even better if he was here with Daisy and not these two cunts. Then he thought, *I'm going to get us back on track. I will get a phone card tonight and give her a bell before I phone home. I will tell her that next year it will be us going away to spend some time together with no cunt getting in our way.*

Just then Jagger kicked open the door with two bags of cold beers. "Room service, lads."

"The beers look cold, mate."

"They are as cold as an Eskimo's dick. Here, get it down you."

"Cheers, Jagger. Now come and see the view."

"What's up, Ringo? You needing a wee kip?"

"Yeah, I think I have jet lag, mate."

"We are only one hour ahead. It's no' as if we went to fucking Alice Springs, mate. Get fucking up and have a beer on the balcony."

As the boys enjoyed the view and the beer, an old couple were sitting on their balcony next door. Mary and Bill were an old couple enjoying retirement maybe getting two or three holidays a year. They both had amazing tans. You could tell sunbathing was the only full-time job they had now.

Mary was a skinny old friendly looking women. She looked like she had lived on coffee and cigarettes all her life. She was all brown skin and bone.

Bill was a big old lad. You could tell he had worked hard with his hands all his life. His big hands were like shovels.

Mary welcomed the boys. "Hello, boys. Are you our new neighbours?"

"Aye, hen. I'm Jagger. This is Syd and our other pal who has got a bit of jet lag is Ringo."

"Jet lag? My God, where are yous boys from?"

"Glasgow."

"I was thinking yous were from somewhere faraway having jet lag."

"I know. It's just our pal has only every travelled to Blackpool his whole life so this is a bit much and he is a wee bit simple."

"I can fucking hear you. I'm tired, no' fucking deaf, dickhead."

"That's him up."

"Well, me and Bill are from Dundee. We like to sit out here and have a wee drink and watch the sun setting. It's lovely."

"Well, we will join yous before we head out for the night."

"That will be good a bit of company because Bill is no' a talker, more a drinker."

"He will get on well with Syd then."

"Bill, the boys will have a drink with us tonight. That will be nice, like a wee party."

"That's good," said Bill as he sipped his whisky.

"We are just going to get ready and powder our nose and that, then we will have a wee drink, hen."

The boys got ready to head out all washed and the room smelt like someone has dropped a bottle of aftershave.

Jagger came out the shower. "Fucking hell, it stinks of Joop in here."

"What did you bring? Old Spice?"

"It would be better than that fucking smell."

"Syd told the boys the lines were ready and Jagger jumped in first.

"Here we go, now it's a holiday."

"Do you think Mary and Bill would like a line?"

"No!"

"Why? They might be into it."

Jagger took a big sniff and stood up in shock. "What the fuck is that?"

"It's coke. It's good stuff, mate."

"My fucking right eyeball is burning. It's about to pop out my head."

"It does look a bit red."

"That's because it's on fire. That's no' coke."

Syd told them, "It's ok. It's because I put my coke in the Askit Powders. You have just got a bit of that."

"Why didn't you take the Askit out of it?"

"I did. Well, most of it anyway."

Ringo went in for a line.

"Did you no' hear me, Ringo? There's Askit mixed in with the coke."

"That's ok. It will help with my hangover in the morning."

Ringo took a line with the boys watching to see his reaction but he was fine.

"How is it?"

"It's good. Now get into it. I'm going to have a beer with Mary and Bill."

As Ringo chatted to Mary, he heard Syd cry, "My fucking eye! It does burn."

"I told you."

"Are your pals ok, son?"

"Yeah, they will be. They just need a good drink down them."

"A few drinks and yous boys will be out on the town, won't they, Bill?"

Yeah, whatever," Bill said without even looking. He just sat there drinking and watching the sun.

Ringo asked, "Does he ever move, Mary?"

"Only if he needs a piss. He just likes to sit in the sun and have a drink."

"It would be cheaper getting him a carry out and taking him for a sun bed, hen."

The boys headed out to the bars near their hotel. They found one that sold cheap beer and they sat outside in the sunshine. Jagger came back from the shops to find the boys had the drinks waiting for him.

"What we got here, lads?"

"When you buy a beer, you get a shot on the house."

"It's a free shot, mate."

"I know what 'on the house' means. Thanks, Ringo."

"What you got there, Jagger?"

"Suncream factor thirty. We'll need it in this heat, lads."

"I won't need it," said Syd.

"You will, mate. Just sitting here for an hour or two will roast us."

"Yeah, Jagger is right, Syd. We are Scots. We are no' white, we are pale blue. We need a week of sunbathing just to go white, then another few days to go brown."

"Listen, boys, I spent my summers in Largs in the hot sun and never once put suncream on. Don't worry."

Jagger went to the bar and came back with a round of drinks and three packets of crisps. Ringo sat smiling at all the girls in the bar.

"Here, Ringo. Beer and crisps."

"No' for me. I'm off the crisps, mate."

"Why?"

"I'm looking after myself. No' wanting to get fat."

"As my da always says, I've seen more fat on a butcher's pencil."

"I know but I haven't had any crisps for two weeks now and it's been a long road. They should do rehab for cunts off the crisps."

"What, like the AA?"

"Aye. People could meet up and say, 'Hi, I'm Ringo and it's been two weeks since my last packet of cheese and onion.'"

Syd said, "Or you could say, 'Hi, I'm Ringo and I'm off the Pringles.'"

"It's no' funny. I can see them in my sleep."

"Well, you're on holiday so fuck it."

"No, I'm no' getting fat now. All the birds in here are looking for a good time."

As the day went by and the night came to meet the boys, they headed into the first club they could find with the free shots with your beer deal. As they stood at the busy bar, the music was pumping and everywhere they looked all they could see were drunk females.

"It's wall to wall with fanny in here, lads," said Ringo. "Syd, you're looking a bit red. You ok?"

"No, I think I have sunburn, boys. I feel like shit."

"A cold beer will sort you out."

"Right, get the beers. I'm away to talk to them birds over at the toilets."

"Syd, if you don't feel well, I will take you back to the hotel."

"No, I'm fine. We will need to keep an eye on Ringo anyway."

"It's no' Ringo we need to worry about. It's the poor bird who gets stuck with him."

Ringo came back over to get his beer, smiling. "Right, boys. The girls over there are going to take us to a better club."

"Who is?"

"Them over there. The four big girls."

"What, the fat birds by the toilets?"

"They are no' that fat."

"They fucking are. They look like they got barred from Slimming World. Fuck's sake, mate."

"Look, this is why we're here."

"No, it isn't, Ringo. I'm here to spend some quality time with my pals, drinking beer and getting a tan."

"They are well up for it, lads. Come on. I mean, look at the one with blonde hair."

"I'm trying not to, mate."

"I'm going to split her like an old bit of firewood."

"Well, see you later. I'm staying here."

"Well, what about you, Syd?"

"Yeah, I'm staying here too, Ringo. We can do better than that."

"Ok, your loss. I'm off."

"Ringo, don't be bringing one of them Teletubbies back to our room."

"How no'? I might let you watch."

"I would rather watch a rat eat my cock than watch you roll about with that big fucking sumo wrestler."

Later that night Ringo found his pals in another club. Jagger was up at the bar looking down into the dance floor.

"All right, Jagger. Where's Syd?"

"He's down there, mate, dancing with some bird."

"He must be feeling better then."

"Yeah, it's amazing what a beer and a line can do."

"Are you sure he's ok? He isn't moving much."

"It's the sunburn, mate. He has been dancing about for the last hour like C-3PO."

"Hope you're staying out. I'm heading back to the hotel."

"No way, big bird. Are you?"

"Hell yes."

"Smashing… fucking smashing."

"You can sit out on the balcony. I won't be long."

"If you don't satisfy her, she will rip your wee dick off."

"Don't worry about me. Just you keep an eye on Syd. He is no' saying much but the guy is hurting bad over this Daisy."

"I know, mate. I was hoping this time away would take his mind off it all but it hasn't."

"Well, watch him. I'm away."

"Have fun, mate."

Jagger helped Syd up the road to the hotel. It took them a while which Jagger didn't mind because the longer they took the better the chance Ringo was done with his one-night stand. As Jagger stood Syd up against the door to open it he could here Ringo going for it.

"Yes, you like that, hen."

"Fuck me, Ringo, fuck me hard, my wee jock."

Jagger took a deep breath, walked into the room, put Syd on his bed, grabbed a beer and ran without looking to the balcony. Ringo still going for it, his wee arse going up and down like a yoyo, giving Jagger the fear.

Out on the balcony Mary and Bill were still up drinking and smoking. "Hi, son."

"All right, Mary. You and Bill still up?"

"Yeah, sounds like you're having a good time."

"Well, Ringo is and Syd no' so much."

"Why? What's up with him?"

"He has a broken heart and sunburn and a cunt of a hangover coming."

"And Ringo?"

"Well, he is doing good. Nothing gets Ringo down."

"And you?"

"I'm good. Just enjoyed my night with my pals."

"Yous must look after each other."

"We do. They are my brothers, my family."

"I ken that, son."

Bill handed Jagger a whisky.

"Thanks, Bill, cheers."

"No worries, son. One for the road, lad, then it's bedtime."

"Yeah, we will keep it down and Ringo will be done any minute now. Don't worry."

Bill downed his large whisky in one then walked away to his bed.

"He is some size, your Bill."

"Yeah, he is, son. Everyone kens him in our toon and no one ever dared to mess with him."

"No wonder. The size of his hands… if he holds a pint I bet it would look like a half pint."

"Aye, he doesn't need to punch anyone. A good slap from him will knock anyone out cold."

"He could maybe slap me so I can get a good night sleep."

"Aye. I have a feeling your pal is keeping you up tonight, Jagger."

"Think you might be right. Anyway, Mary, I'm away in to deal with them. See you tomorrow."

"Aye, goodnight, son."

The next day, late in the afternoon, the boys hit the pool.

"Time to get my tan on, lads."

"You already have a tan, Jagger. You're a sunbed junkie."

"I know but need to top it up and I feel like shit so I'm hoping the sun helps."

"You got a hangover?"

"A wee bit but I think I'm in for the cold."

"How the fuck can you get the cold in the sun?"

"Easy, Ringo. You get it through germs like when some cunt brings back a Teletubby with a cough to your room and now I feel like shit."

"It's a hangover, no' a cold. A wee cocktail and you will be brand new. Syd, what you want to drink?"

"A beer, Ringo."

"Cool, so that's a beer, a sex on the beach and a Lemsip for Jagger."

As Ringo got back with the drinks, Syd jumped in the pool with a rubber ring they got at the shops.

The lifeguard walked over to them. He was a wee guy with a bit of a belly and a hump on his back. "Sir, no ring in the pool, ok?"

"Why? I'm only going to sit in it and chill."

"No, sir. No allowed in the pool, ok?"

"Then why the fuck they selling them in the hotel shop then?"

"You take to the beach, no the pool, ok? I no tell you again."

"All right, Hasselhoff. Chill, mate."

The wee lifeguard walked back to his seat, still watching the boys.

"See that prick? He needs to get a job. He likes giving us a hard time for fuck all."

"I know. How the fuck is he a lifeguard? Wee fat cunt with a hump."

"I bet his mum got him a wok for his birthday."

"Why a wok, Ringo?"

"So he could iron his shirts, mate."

"Don't worry, they swap round every hour so he will be gone soon for a bit."

"Yeah, the blonde bird will be here next. I seen her at the bar."

"Blonde? Is she good looking?"

"She's ok."

"Blonde lifeguard sounds like Pamela Anderson."

"No, mate, I wish. She looks more like Pamela from Anderson."

As the day got hotter the boys kept drinking to cool down. As they sat in the sun and burnt the boys didn't say much. They were just enjoying the hangovers leaving them as the beers and cocktails sunk in.

Ringo kept asking what the plans for tonight were because he was worried his pals had forgotten what day it was. And they had. In all the madness of the drink and the coke from last night they had forgotten that it was Ringo's birthday. But not just any birthday. It his twenty-first. The whole reason they came out here.

"Lads, what are we doing again tonight?"

"For the hundredth time, Ringo. We will go out, get drunk and take drugs. And maybe Syd will dance like fucking C-3PO again."

"Cool, lads. Sounds good."

"Yep, Ringo, we can't wait."

"I will get the drinks in, boys."

Syd asked Jagger, "What the fuck is up with him today?"

"I don't know but he is doing my nut in going on and on about tonight."

"There is something no' right but I can't put my finger on it."

73

"Oh fucking suck ma dick, we have forgotten about his fucking birthday."

"Shit, it's today?"

"Aye, mate. We need to think fast."

"Ok, let's ask the hotel for a cake."

"Syd, he's twenty-one, no' fucking twelve."

"Ok, then what?"

"We will say we're going to the shop for fags and we will find him a hooker."

"Ok, cool. Here he comes."

"Cold beers, lads. Dig in."

"Cheers, Ringo."

"Hey, Syd, you got any smokes on you?"

"Who? Me? No, I need to go to the shop."

"I have fags here, lads."

"No, it's ok. We'll need more for tonight. We'll just down our beers and go and get some. You can watch the towels, mate."

"Ok, I get it, lads. Yeah, I will stay here."

Jagger and Syd headed out onto the strip.

"Ok, Syd. We will split up and meet back here in thirty minutes."

"Cool, so what am I looking for?"

"A fucking dirty cow, mate."

"Yeah, ok. A good looking hooker."

"She doesn't need to be good looking. It's Ringo we are talking about."

"Aye, cool. A dirty hooker who works the afternoon shift. That should be easy."

The boys headed into the busy street hoping to find a lovely good looking dirty hooker for their pal's big day.

About twenty-five minutes later Jagger shouted to Syd from over the road. "Syd, over here, mate."

"Any luck, Jagger?"

"Yes, my old mate found one in this bar and she is up for it."

"Show me."

"Ok, in here. Let's get a beer."

As they got a beer the hooker walked over to them. She was tanned with big tits and long legs. She said she was forty-four but the boys knew she was a bit older.

"Ok, Jagger honey, where you wanting to fuck?"

"No, it's no' me. It's my pal."

Syd looked her up and down.

"You ok there, big boy? You like what you see? You want to fuck?"

"No, I'm good, thanks. Like my pal says, it's our other pal who is up for it." Syd looked down again and asked, "Is that red high-heel shoes you have on?"

"*Si*, why?"

"No, it's just the last time I seen red shoes on a bird there was a house on top of her."

"I don't get it, honey."

"He's talking about the fucking *Wizard of Oz*. Look, never mind him. Are you ok to go to our hotel room and wait for our friend to show up?"

"Ok, let go. I love him long time, baby."

The boys showed the lady to their room and then ran down to the pool to get Ringo. When they got to the pool Ringo was sitting beside a young and very beautiful blonde haired, blue eyed and great wee titted lady.

"All right, lads. This is Emily here. Jagger, her old man is a Stones fan."

"That's good, Ringo, and nice to meet you, dear."

Syd asked Ringo to help him at the bar. "All right, mate. Me and Jagger need you to go to the room and get your birthday present."

"Fucking hell, mate. I was thinking you had forgot about it."

"Us? No chance. How could we forget it's our best pal's birthday. Now head up and open your gift, mate."

"No, I will open it later. I seem to be doing good with this wee Emily bird."

"No, you need to go now, mate. You can fall in love later with Emily."

Jagger walked over. "What's up?"

"He won't go to the room for his gift."

"Why no'?"

"Because he is too busy with wee Emily big tits over there."

"You move your hole and get up to that room, Ringo. I'm no' fucking about here. Time is ticking."

"But I think me and this wee Emily are going somewhere, lads."

"You are going somewhere. You're going up the fucking stairs, mate."

"When you get back down after you're done with your gift, you can spend all day with wee Emily. Now move."

"What is waiting up there for me?"

"You will see when you move your hole."

"Is it a hooker?"

"Might be."

"I don't think I could fuck a hooker right now, lads."

"Why no'?"

"I'm no' sure if I want to do that. You know, cheat on Emily."

"You're no' fucking cheating because she is no' your bird yet."

"Fucking hell, Ringo. Jagger is right. You have just met her. You've known that beer in your hand longer than her."

"Ok, lads. I will go but I can't promise anything like getting your money's worth. No' with the feeling I'm having for wee Emily."

The boys sat back down and chilled in the sun with a beer.

"How much was the hooker, Jagger?"

"Thirty pounds, mate. She didn't want pesetas. She wanted pounds."

"Why she no' want pesetas?"

"No' sure, mate. She said pounds is better and, get this, she also said if I made it fifty pounds he could stick it up her back door."

"Dirty cow. She didn't say that."

"She did, mate, but I told her, 'No, thanks. My pal might be a cunt but he is no' a dirty cunt.'"

"Just as well you didn't pay the extra now that he is in love with wee blonde big tits over there."

"Aye. You can see why Ringo is falling for her. She is smoking hot."

"Aye, I bet the lifeguard would let her play with her ring in the pool."

Ringo walked into his room. "Hello, hen. I'm Ringo. Take it you're my birthday present."

"*Si*, Bingo. Now, let's go. I'm a busy woman."

"It's Ringo, no' Bingo."

"Sorry?"

"Never mind. Let's do this, hen."

"Ok. You want on top or bottom"

"Whatever. I'm good. Now let's get down with the clown."

"Ok, Bingo, you big boy. You fuck me now."

As Ringo was getting in about the hooker, she asked him, "Ok, Bingo, you want to fuck me from behind like woof woof?"

"Did you just say 'woof woof', hen? Fucking hell, I love this Spanish dirty talk."

"*Si*, Bingo. You go fast for me."

"Eyes down for a full house, Bingo is going in."

About fifteen minutes later Ringo came back down to the pool.

"Fucking hell, Ringo. You were quick, mate."

"No, really, I showed her a good time."

"What, did you show her the way out?"

"It must've took you five minutes to get to the room and back."

"I fucked her and I had a shower. I didn't want to come back down here smelling of old hooker."

"I hope you didn't leave her in our room or she will be away with our duty free."

"And our passports."

"You think I'm daft? No. I made sure she left with me."

"Good. Now you can go and fall in love with wee big tits."

"That's the plan, boys. And before I go, that hooker is waiting for you at reception, Jagger."

"Why is she waiting for me?"

"I don't know. She said something about you owe her twenty pounds, mate. Bye."

"Smashing!" Jagger shouted as Ringo walked away laughing.

Later that day Ringo came back with a round of drinks for his pals. "Here we go, lads. Get them while they're cold."

Jagger sat up holding his back.

"You ok, Jagger?"

"Yes, mate. It's just these beds. They get my back stiffer than a honeymoon cock."

"I know how you feel, mate, and this heat is killing me."

Syd sat up. "We can't complain about the heat. That is why we're here."

"We know, Syd, but it's hotter than a Mexican whorehouse today."

"It is today. Ringo is sweating like a whore in church."

"I'm sweating and I put on Syd's Lynx Africa and still I'm like a burst pipe."

Syd looked and noticed Jagger had a good watch on. "Never seen you with that watch, mate. Where did you get it?"

"Aye, Jagger, that looks really nice."

"Yeah, this watch, I don't wear it much and I didn't mean to bring it with me. I was in that much of a hurry I picked up the wrong watch. My old man gave it to me. It was my granddad's watch and even his dad passed it to him so it's old, real old.

"My great granddad gave it to his son who was going away to war. You know, it was in the time of the Second World War. He told my dad he was saying goodbye to his family but his dad wasn't saying much, then as he got to the train station his dad handed him this watch and told him, 'Son, I got two of these watches and they both tell the same time. So when it hits midnight and you're feeling scared or alone, just look up at the stars and the moon and know I will be looking too at the same time so you will never be alone.' And he told my dad he did and it helped him get through the war.

"And after he passed away my dad got the watch. And I always remember we were away on a family holiday to Blackpool when I was wee and my old man took us up the Blackpool Tower and he was steaming. My mum was wanting to go back to the B&B but my dad was wanting to get up and sing. And I was wanting to stay because there was a magic act coming on. So we are sitting there. I'm in heaven having a glass bottle of Coke and crisps and the magician asks for a volunteer and my drunk arse da gets up."

"Your ma must have been real happy about that."

"She was wanting to hide under the fucking table. So he asked my da for his watch and as he gives it to him, my da tells him, 'Look, this watch means a lot to me.' And the magician is like, 'Don't worry, sir, and tell everyone where you are from, sir.' It's like the guy is no' giving a fuck. He is too busy to listen to my da. He is trying to keep the crowd happy.

"Next thing the old gold watch is put in a wee velvet bag and he fucks it with a hammer. My old da, he was about to pass out then the magician waves his hand and says some daft shit and puts the bag upside down and the watch falls out into a million fucking bits."

At the same time, Ringo and Syd both said, "Fuck off."

"I'm telling you, lads. My old man is about to kill the cunt right there up on the stage. So my mum is like, 'We need to go. Your dad is about to get the jail,' but my da goes away to the side of the stage to talk to the tower manager. My dad comes back and says, 'They are taking us to some restaurant to work out how much to pay me for the watch.'

"My mum says, 'We are no' going. I'm going back to the B&B.' My da is like, 'We are fucking going.' My mum says, 'You just want money and a few free drinks.' So we get took in a taxi to this restaurant and the magician is sitting waiting at a big table for us. He says, 'Hi again. I am very sorry about the watch.' My da tells him, 'My grandad had that watch in the war and you can't put a price on it.'"

"And did he give your da loads of cash and he got you that gold watch?"

"No. We were sitting there and my da was getting a lot of free whisky. When the food arrived the magician looked at me and said, 'You like lasagne, son?' I said, 'Don't know. Never had it.' And he says, 'Dig in. I think you and your dad will be happy with it.' And when I put the folk in you will never guess what was in the fucking lasagne."

"Ringo jumped up off his sun bed and shouted, "Your granddad's watch!"

"No, mate. Mince."

Syd looked at Jagger in shock. "It never fucking happened, did it?"

"No," laughed Jagger. "I got it today off one of the 'looky looky' guys when we were looking for a hooker for him."

"You dirty fucker, Jagger. You fucking had us there, mate."

"Sorry, boys. Let me buy you a beer to make it up to yous."

"I will take a gold watch if you can go and find another one, thanks," said Syd.

It was the last day of the boys' time away and as they were in their room packing and still drinking, Jagger came out the shower. "Anyone no' had a wash yet? Because there is no more hot water."

"I just need to get my hair and that's me good to go. Syd, get the last of the beers out the fridge, mate."

"Cool, well, here we go, lads. One for the road."

"Fuck talking about one for the road, we better say goodbye to Mary and Bill."

Ringo headed to the bathroom to fix his hair as Jagger and Syd went out onto the balcony. "They're no' out here."

"Fuck. That's a first. They sit out here all day and night."

"When do they leave?"

"I don't know, Syd. I'm no' their holiday rep, mate."

Just as they were talking, the boys heard a squeaking sound coming from Mary and Bill's rooms. Jagger looked at Syd, his face in shock.

"They are doing it."

"Doing what?"

"What do you think?"

"What, *it*?"

"Well, they are no' doing the fucking hokey cokey."

"No, they can't be. The size of Bill… he would kill her."

"Well, they are on holiday and drinking which will always lead to sex."

"I know, but they're old."

"Old cunts still fuck. I mean, Ringo's granny has a boyfriend."

"Does she?"

"Yeah, but he doesn't like to talk about it so don't say anything."

"Strange days, mate. Remember when your granny was just a wee nice old lady going to the bingo now they have boyfriends."

"Strange days indeed, mate. Strange days indeed."

Ringo walked out onto the balcony. "What the fuck is happening here, boys?"

Jagger whispered, "Mary and Bill are fucking."

"No, they're no'."

"They are, mate. The bed is squeaking."

"Mary is too old to be fucking."

"No, Jagger says old people fuck now."

"What the fuck do yous mean by that? Yous two have better no' have been talking about my granny."

Syd looked at him trying not to laugh. "Why would we be talking about your granny?"

"Because she has a male friend and a lot of cunts think it's her boyfriend."

"Is he your step-granddad?"

"No, Jagger, he fucking isn't, ok?"

"Wait, I can hear the bed again."

Ringo told them, "Look, they can't be fucking because that cunt Bill is a big lad. The other day I seen him pulling up his shorts out here and let's just say from what I seen he is a big lad. A very big lad."

"Did he show you it like, 'Here, son, how do you like them apples.'?"

"No, funny cunt. He didn't see me but I seen him unfortunately. And his dick was longer than the last hour of a night shift."

"Yeah, Ringo is right, Jagger. Old Bill would split her in two. A wee old women like her and him trying to fuck would be like sticking King Kong's thumb up her."

"Yeah, maybe you're right, lads. They might be just packing too."

"Yes, packing sounds better in my head than seeing them fucking. That's sick."

Just as the boys were about to walk back into their room, they heard old Mary shout, "Tack it oot, Bill ! Tack it oot.

You're hurting me. Jesus Christ, Bill. It's too big. You're ripping me wide!"

The boys looked at each other in shock and ran into their room laughing.

Jagger grabbed his bag. "We need to get out of here. I can't look Mary and Bill in the face."

Ringo sat on the bed. "That poor wee woman. He was killing her. That's no' right."

Syd asked Ringo, "Do you think that's how your granny sounds with her friend?"

"No, she doesn't, dickhead. She only goes to the bingo with him, no' on fucking holiday."

"Should we go back out and make sure she is ok?"

"She will be fine. She will be having a smoke now. Let's go. We have a plane to catch, lads."

CHAPTER 5

IDLE HANDS AND NO PLANS...

A few days later Ringo and Syd sat in the pub waiting for Jagger to finish his shift. The two of them sat there, sad faces on, having the holiday blues. Back to the same old shit waiting on another winter now their one week of summer was over.

"Even the beer is no' doing it for me just now. It's no' the same somehow."

"It's because of the little difference in the surroundings, Ringo."

"Like what?"

"Like sitting by the pool in the hot sun and all them young hot birds in bikinis. That makes a big difference, mate."

"Yeah, it's better than in here with old Archie sleeping beside me. I'm sure he has shit himself."

"No, he hasn't. You can smell Del the Smell. He has just walked in with his fat bird."

"I'm no' in the mood for that cunt today."

Del walked right over to the boys. "All right, lads. Any weed?"

"Yes, we have Smell—I mean, Del, but you still owe us money from last week, cunt."

"Yeah, lads, I will be getting my giro tomorrow so I will pay you all of it then."

"Good, Del, and then we will give you more weed tomorrow then."

"Why can't I get a bit today, lads?"

"Because, Del, my good friend, Ringo should have never given you a bit on tick in the first place."

"Why no'?"

"I'm no' in the mood today, Del, but if it makes you fuck off away from my table I will tell you. You see, we don't do tick because if we did it would piss off the money lenders and I don't want to piss them cunts off."

"But they take fuck all to do with your drugs."

"That's right, Del, but we deal, we don't lend. That's how it works. You go and lend money from them and you come to us to buy drugs. If we give out tick, they don't make fuck all."

"Ringo gave me it on tick because he is a friend."

"No, Del. I gave you it so I didn't need to carry it through the airport."

"You see, Del, this what we do. It's a job, We don't sit in here talking to cunts like you for fun. No, it's work, mate. It's how we make money."

Jagger and fat Annmarie walked in the door at the same time.

Ringo shouted, "Hey, Jagger. Is that you and Annmarie just up?"

"Fuck up, Ringo, and just you sit there. I will get the beers."

Annmarie walked over to the table. "Did you get some, honey?"

"No, they don't do tick."

"Why?"

"Because he needs to get money off the money lenders."

"But we owe them, we can't go to them."

"That sounds like a you problem, hen."

"Fuck up, Ringo, or I will tell everyone in here you have a wee baby dick."

"You would love to get a hold of my dick, hen."

"I did get hold of it. With my finger and thumb. It was that wee."

Jagger walked over with the beers. "Del, take your smell away from here before it knocks me out and then I will have to knock you the fuck out."

"I was just wanting a bit of weed, Jagger."

"Do you have money for it?"

"No, mate."

"Then fuck off."

As Del and fat Ammo were walking away she turned and said, "It hurts me when you tell people we didn't fuck, Ringo. I will never forget that night we had together. It reminded me of Christmas."

"What, really?"

"Yes, your dick was like a wee pigs in blankets."

Jagger downed his beer almost in one.

"Were you needing that, mate?"

"Yes, Syd. It was a long day in work. I think I have the holiday blues."

"Me too, mate. I can't get my ass in gear."

"It will take it out of you, mate, sitting about in here selling drugs all day. Nightmare. How is you and Daisy getting on?"

"Good. I took her out for dinner and gave her the holiday gifts I got her. She was looking happy to see me."

"And what about her mum and dad?"

"They're still giving her a hard time about me."

"They need to chill out."

"It's no' that it's some cunt in her dad's work told them about us and what we get up to. And they want us to spilt and her no' to work in here anymore."

"She has to choose them or you, mate, and if it's you then you will need to get a flat with her."

"I would love that, mate, but we will see. I will get the beers."

"Right, Ringo, while Syd is at the bar, I need a favour from you."

"Sure. What you need?"

"Do you know that cunt Paul Gallagher?"

"No, mate. Who is he?"

"He drinks in that shithole the Black Swan."

"That is a shithole. My old man got slashed in there years ago."

"Well, he owes me money and he has been dodging me, the cunt."

"If we go to get him in the Black Swan, we will need to be tooled up."

"No, I've found out the cunt's address so we can get him there late tomorrow night."

"Is Syd coming?"

"No, his head is up his arse with all this Daisy shit. It will be just me and you and bring a tool."

"Why if he doesn't give you the money? Are we doing him?"

"Yeah, I will hit him but I just want him to see you tooled up so he will shit himself and pay up."

"Ok, I will find something that will scare the shit out of him."

"A hammer or a big bat will be good. The cunt will pay up and then we will head into the night."

Syd came back from the bar with the beers. "Guys, I'm telling yous, I have been feeling like shit since we got back."

"I'm the same, Syd. It's the air in the plane that fucks you up, mate."

"You might be right, Ringo, but it will never stop us going on holiday."

"Yep, you can't beat a wee drink on the plane. Gets you in the mood."

"I like a wee gin and tonic on the plane."

"I noticed that. Jagger, what the fuck is that all about? You're a Jack D man."

"I don't know. Different places… I like a different drink. You know, like at Christmas I like a Bailey's but I would never drink it in here or a cocktail in the sun."

"Syd likes that. Just he has it without the tail."

"Funny cunt, Ringo. I like dark rum sometimes if I have a bad hangover."

"A good whisky for me when I have a hangover but only one or two when you have a busy day ahead like an all-day wedding."

"Sounds good. Let's get one just now."

"Why? You going to a wedding today, Ringo?"

"No, I just want to see if it works. I have a wee hangover just now."

"I wish we were on that plane just now, having a wee Jack Daniels and Coke, lads."

"Jagger would still have a fucking G&T thinking he is 007."

"James Bond drank vodka martinis, dickhead."

"It's mad to think about it all. Them cunts on that plane and it gets up in the air."

"You're right, Ringo. It is mad when you think about it. Like two hundred people, all the cases, all the food and drink and we shoot through the sky at that speed. It's nuts."

"It's an amazing thing. People are impressive with what they come up with."

"It was Howard Hughes. He was one of the first guys to say people would travel in the sky and everyone said he was nuts."

"Because he was nuts. He kept his own piss in jars and in the end lived alone."

"He was still a brilliant man."

Jagger asked a question. "What do you think is the best invention ever?"

Ringo said, "The toaster."

Jagger spit his beer out. "What? The fucking toaster?"

"Yeah, where would we be without it?"

"So, out of all the inventions and the fact that the Scots are known as the best in the world at inventions, you are saying the fucking toaster?"

"Yep."

"Ringo, I will try and say this in one breath, ok? What about televisions, telephones, penicillin, MRI scanners, refrigerators, cash machines, the flushing toilet, syringes, fingerprints, and the stamp. And that's just a few."

"Well, that's pretty good but I'm still sticking with the toaster, lads."

"So, why the toaster, Ringo? Tell us."

"Where would we be without it? All of us are made of toast. It was the only thing we got to eat as kids. No food in the house but if you had a loaf of bread it went a long way."

"You could say the same thing about homemade soup."

"Good point, Syd, but the toaster stopped people from being late for work and school. Think about it. If we all got up to fried eggs and bacon we would always be running late. But if we pop some bread in the toaster we are out the door in no time with a hot slice of toast in our hands ready for the day ahead. And the best part about it is when you pop the bread down, if it hasn't been switched on at the wall, it will just pop back up. Now that's smart."

"I really don't know what to say to that. You blow my mind, Ringo."

"Also..."

"Fuck, there's more."

"Is that why Doc Brown in *Back to the Future* always says, 'Great Scots,' because we were so good at inventions?"

"No, mate. That's about some Scots guy who was too fat to sit on his horse or some shit like that, but you could be onto something there, mate."

The next night Jagger was standing at the side of the pub. It was dark and pissing down with rain and that was the way he wanted it to be. If it was cold and wet then there would be less people about. As he stood in the shadows, Ringo showed up.

"Bang on time, Ringo. Good man."

"Don't worry, Jagger. I don't know much but I know the meaning of the word pals."

"I know you do, mate. Now let's walk."

"Who stays with this Paul Gallagher?"

"No' sure. His bird and a few kids? But at this time of night they should be in their beds."

"Good. Last thing we need is some bird screaming fucking blue murder."

"Did you bring a tool?"

"Yeah, mate, don't worry. I got a tool."

"Good, but remember, you don't need it. I don't want to do him. I want my money."

"Don't worry, Jagger. We will get your money."

"You saying that is what makes me worry, Ringo. Ok, you stay here at the gate and don't say a word."

"Cool. I will just stand here under the streetlight in the rain looking badass."

Jagger went and chapped on the door. A guy came to the door in his shorts and vest looking surprised to see Jagger.

"Evening, Paul."

"All right, Jagger. I was going to come and see you, mate."

"Funny, because I have been trying to get a hold of you for the last few weeks, cunt."

"Coming to my door is a bit much, Jagger. My wife and kids are in bed."

"Don't fucking put that on me. You were the one no' answering my phone calls, getting your wife to talk to me and do your dirty work."

"Who's your pal, Jagger?"

"Never mind him. You will get to know him well enough if you don't have my fucking money."

"I can get it, mate."

"Good. Go and get it then."

"Well, I can't get it tonight. Maybe next week."

"Fuck next week, Paul. I want my money now."

"No can do, mate."

"No can do? What the fuck does that mean? Ringo says it means no tin pigeon."

Paul laughed. "Good one, mate."

"You think this is fucking funny, Paul?"

"No, Jagger. I will get you the money tomorrow. I will bring it to the pub you drink in. What's it called again?"

"It's the Argosy bar and I will be there waiting for you at 6 p.m. Don't be fucking late."

"Right, 6 p.m. Yeah, I will be there."

Just as Jagger was about to leave, Ringo ran up the path, pushed past Jagger and pulled out his old man's sawed off shotgun. He grabbed Paul out away from his door and put the gun on his chin. "Now you listen to me, cunt. If you don't show up tomorrow and leave us sitting about like cunts, I will come back here in the middle of the night and fucking finish you. Then I will go to your funeral and give your wife a shoulder to cry on."

Paul shit his shorts. "Fucking ok, mate. Chill. You don't need to this. I will get the fucking money, mate."

He ran into his house locking the door behind him.

Jagger stood in shock.

"Come on, Jagger. Let's walk, mate."

As they headed into the dark, Jagger asked him, "Where the fuck did you get that, Ringo?"

"It's my old man's. He's had it for years."

"If that cunt goes to the cops they will kick our doors in tonight."

"He won't go to the cops. He'll pay up."

"Let me see that."

"Why?"

"Because I want to see it. Get a hold of it."

"Ok but he careful."

"Fuck me it's old."

"Yeah, he got it years back when he was up to no good as a boy."

"And now you are up to no good with it."

"No, I just took it for tonight."

"Bullshit. You've done a few shops with this, haven't you?"

"No, have I fuck."

"You have had a bit of extra money here and there, Ringo. I'm no' daft."

"So fucking what? I got away with it so far."

"Yeah, but for how long? If the cops get you one time with this they will match you to all the other times and you will be fucked, mate."

"Well, they won't unless we just stand here in the pissing rain waiting for them to show up."

"One good thing is that it's so old it won't work anyway."

"This can still do some damage, mate."

"It will damage cunts' pants when you shove it in there face, maybe."

"I'm telling you it will do the job and God help the cunt that gets on the wrong side of me or my pals."

"Chill, Billy the Kid."

"Fuck you. It works and that's that. Now can we fucking go?"

"Ok, mate, cool. Go and put that wherever the fuck you found it and meet me tomorrow in the pub. I will buy you a few beers when I get my money."

"Smashing."

"And, Ringo… thanks for tonight."

"What are pals for, Jagger?"

The next night Jagger and Ringo were sitting in the pub having a beer waiting for Paul to show up with the money. At the bar there was a group of girls getting drunk.

"Hey, Jagger. Check out the birds at the bar."

"I see them, Ringo."

"You think they're out for the night?"

"Yep, looks like a works night out. Maybe someone's birthday."

"Yeah, my birthday with a bit of luck."

"You stay on the clock, Ringo. We're here to get the money, no' go on a fucking hen do."

"I know. Don't worry. That cunt Paul will show up and pay up, mate, and then we can have a drink with the girls."

"Yeah, you can. I'm going to meet Sally. It's date night."

"Date night? What the fuck? How can you go on a date with the bird you stay with?"

"It's no' a date. It's just a way of spending time together away from everyone else."

"Where you going?"

"Into that new pub in town."

"I've been told it's really good in there. Can I come?"

"No, mate. If you come then it's no' date night, is it?"

"I could pull one of them birds and bring her."

"No, but which one would you go for anyway?"

"That wee blonde. She is fit as fuck."

"Yeah, she is no' bad."

"No' bad? She is hot. Fucking King Arthur couldn't pull me out of her."

"You're a sick man, Ringo."

Just as the boys were talking, the door opened but it was only Syd walking in. "All right, lads. What's happening?"

"No' much. You want a beer, Syd?"

"Yes. Cheers, Ringo. You didn't look happy to see me, mate."

"No, we're waiting for a cunt who has money for me. We dug him last night. He should be here any minute now."

"What we up to tonight then?"

"I'm going for a drink with Sally. Sorry, mate, you're drinking with Ringo and them girls over there."

"Where you going for a drink?"

"That new pub in town."

"Sounds good. Can we come?"

"Fucking hell, no. It's date night, no' bring a mate night, Syd."

"Ok, chill."

Ringo came back with the drinks as Paul walked in with a bag in his hand.

"Take a seat, Paul. You're late."

"Well, I couldn't find this shithole."

"Easy, Paul. Don't talk about our pub, mate. Even if it is a shithole, it's our shithole."

"Yeah, ok. Do you think I could maybe get a beer in your pub?"

"No. You're no' staying, mate."

"Hi, Paul," Ringo said, "You sleep well last night?"

"You stay away from me, you wee cunt."

"No need for that, Paul. What's wrong?"

"What's wrong is you coming to my door with a fucking—"

"Keep your voice down, Paul."

"Fucking no' right that the cheese has slipped off your cracker, mate."

"Look, pal, just pay up and fuck off," said Syd.

"Who the fuck are you?"

"I'm a cunt who is no' in the mood for cunts like you, so pay my pal and go."

"Here, Jagger. It's all there and don't come to my door again."

"I won't, Paul, because I will never deal with you again."

Paul stood up. "I'm away for a real pint in a better pub than this."

"The Black Swan is a shithole."

"Yeah, well, maybe. If you had come looking for me in the Swan my pals wouldn't have let you back out alive."

Syd jumped and kicked Paul right between the legs and Paul hit the floor.

"Bull's-eye!" Ringo shouted before sipping his pint.

Jagger looked down at Paul. "You need to go, mate, now before you get really hurt."

The boys watched him climb up the table and hold his balls, walking out the door.

"Sorry about that, Jagger, but he was doing my head in."

"That's ok, Syd. He was asking for it."

"You hit that cunt so hard in the balls he will be talking like one of the Bee Gees for the next few weeks."

"Right, lads. I'm having this beer then I'm away to meet Sally. Now try and stay out of trouble for one night and I will see yous tomorrow."

"Aye. Enjoy date night, Jagger."

A few hours later Jagger met Sally in a bar in town for date night.

"How was work?" Jagger asked her.

"Shit as always. How was your day? Did you get your money back from that guy?"

"Yep and now I'm going to spend it on you tonight, honey."

"Good. It's about time it was just you and me for a bit."

"Tonight I'm all yours."

"So where is Syd and Ringo?"

"In the pub chatting up a group of birds."

"Daisy will no' be happy if she is on shift tonight."

"No, Syd says her mum and dad want her to give up working in the pub so she might no' be back."

"How is Syd taking it?"

"He is going out his way to keep her happy and I hope it works out or he will be heartbroken."

"I'm sure they will work it out. Syd just needs to stop going drinking with Ringo every night."

"I know. I told him that it's no' good."

"What you talking about? You have been out with them and phoning in sick with hangovers."

"I'm just trying to keep my mate busy, that's all."

"Yeah, you're a real hero, Jagger."

"Got to look after my pals, Sally."

"What about all that shit with the Crow?"

"That's old news. It's over."

"I hope so."

"It is. The Crow has forgot about all that by now. He is a busy man."

"As you and your pals always say, he is nuttier than squirrel shit."

"He is, but he will just move on. He won't have any beef with me. Trust me."

"I hate when you say, 'Trust me.' It gives me the fear, Jagger."

"As long as wee Leeann is ok and he stays away from her then it's all good."

"You're no' her dad, Jagger."

"I know that. It was just no' right, her getting with him."

"I know, but we can't tell her what to do. She will find her own way in life."

Sally went to the bar to get the drinks in when the pub door opened and who walked in but Syd, Ringo and a bunch of very drunk girls.

Sally looked over at Jagger. "Great, there goes date night."

"Jagger, my brother," Ringo shouted. "I have been telling our new pals here all about you and Sally so they wanted to say hello."

"Hello, girls. Now goodbye, boys."

"Come on, mate. Don't be like that. Let's have a drink."

Ringo went to the bar to buy Sally a drink and Syd sat down with Jagger.

"What the fuck, Syd?"

"What? The girls were heading into town and Ringo was going with them no matter what, so I had to come."

"Why here?"

"It's the first pub you pass from the bus stop, mate."

"Smashing."

Ringo came over with a load of shots. "Here we go, guys. If you can't get them down you then get them up you."

"No' like you to be in the toon at night, Ringo. You don't like it, do you?"

"No, but all these pretty girls talked me into it."

Sally asked, "Why does he no' like it?"

"Never mind Jagger, Sally. He's just trying to be funny."

"Funny about what? Jagger, why doesn't he like it?"

"Because—"

"Don't start, Jagger."

"Come on, Ringo. It was a fun night."

"What was a fun night? Syd, you tell me please."

"We came into the toon a few years back and it was all good till Ringo got hold of some ecstasy pills. We took one each and they were strong. We were out our nuts."

"Yep and the rest of the night was a fucking blur. End of. Now who wants a drink?"

"Wait a minute. What about when we were kicked out the pub walking about lost out of our heads?"

"And what happened then?"

"Well, we were told to get out the pub because we were no' buying drinks. So, we left and walked into the cold dark night."

"Yeah, the three of us were just walking about cold and lost and we got to this club and two guys at the door asked us if we were ok and we told them the truth."

"What, that you had taken ecstasy?"

"Aye and they were like, 'Hey, that's cool. You've come to the right place, boys. Come on in.' And we told them, 'No, we don't want a drink.' And they says, 'In here you don't drink, honey, you dance.'"

"Oh my fucking God, was it a gay bar?"

"Hell yes it was a gay bar."

"And did you go in?"

"Yep. Full of ecstasy. It sounded like a great idea."

"Right, that's plenty," said Ringo.

"Did yous dance?"

"Yep, we were up on the floor all night."

"I would have loved to have seen that."

"The best part was they asked our names and then they wanted to know the story behind our nicknames and so as the night went on they gives us nicknames."

"Can you remember them?"

"No, we can't," said Ringo.

"I can," said Syd.

"What were they, Syd?"

"Well, Jagger was Ebeneezer Goode because he had the pills. I was Elton John because of my glasses."

"And what was Ringo?"

"Small town boy."

"That's right, Jagger. You gave away our pills."

"One was plenty, Ringo. We were out our nut."

"Yeah and some of them were a bit too friendly."

"All I remember was they played some good tunes that night. We should go tonight."

"Hell no."

As the night went on, the girls they were with were leaving. Sally took a taxi with them as there was not enough room for the boys.

"I will get a lift up the road with the girls and put a good word in for Ringo."

"Make sure they drop you right at the flat. Don't be walking home."

"I won't. Don't worry. You get a beer and the last train. I will see you at home."

"Cool, ok."

"And Jagger…"

"Yeah?"

"Remember what I said."

"What?"

"We need some time. Just you and me."

"We will. Don't worry."

The boys sat and had another beer.

"Just one more beer then I'm off to get the train, lads."

"One more? Fuck that. We can get the last train in two hours or so."

"You're forgetting, Ringo, I'm on a promise. It's date night, mate."

"Fuck me, I'm sorry I want to spend time with my pals."

"That's all we do, Ringo."

"I know, but it won't be forever, lads."

"You've had too many shots, Ringo."

"I know, mate. I just miss the old days of getting up to no good when we were wee guys."

"We still get up to no good, mate."

"Jagger, remember the Afghan melon?"

"Fuck me, Ringo. That takes me back. The fucking Afghan melon."

Syd asked, "What's the Afghan melon?"

"It was a Billy Connolly joke about some cunt asking the guy on the fruit and veg van if the melon he was selling was Afghan because he was reading a cookbook."

"Aye. Jagger would watch it all the time. So much that we decided it could work in shops to rob. You know, we would go in, ask for a few cans of beer, a bottle of whisky, a packet of fags and then we would ask them."

"Ask them what?"

"We would say, 'Excuse me. Them melons you're selling. Are they Afghan or honeydew?' The daft cunt would say, 'I'm no' sure,' and we would roll our eyes and say, 'Can you go and ask someone who does know please?' And as soon as they went in to the back of the shop to ask the manager, we were off out the door with the beer and the whisky and the smokes."

"Yep, too easy."

"But what if the shop didn't sell melons?"

"That was easy too. We would just get the drink and smokes then ask for something from the back of the shop. Anything as long as it was far away from the counter. We would be like, 'I almost forgot my mum needs some lemonade as well please.' And as soon as he was at the back of the shop picking it up we were gone."

"The Afghan melon swindle."

"Yeah. God, I love Billy Connolly."

Late that night the boys dropped off a very drunk Jagger in a taxi because they had missed the last train.

"Night night, boys."

"See you tomorrow, Jagger."

"Aye, Jagger. See you tomorrow. And by the way, I'm pretty sure date night is out the window, mate."

"No shit, Sherlock."

Jagger walked up to his flat trying to be quiet. When he got the door open, the flat was in darkness. He walked into the bedroom ready for his grilling from Sally. He looked at the bed in the dark and he couldn't see her so he put the light on. She was not in bed so he went to the front room. She was not there either, so he shouted her name but no one was home.

"Where the fuck is she?"

He looked at the time. It was 1 a.m. He was starting to sober up trying to work out where she could be. He phoned her mum's house but there was no answer. *That cunt will be too drunk to wake up,* he thought. He then phoned the hospital but her name didn't show up.

He sat alone on the floor in the dark till 5 a.m. when he finally fell asleep.

At 8:30 a.m. the phone rang. It was Sally's mum.

"Is Sally there, Jagger?"

"No, I tried to phone you last night. She hasn't come home."

"What do you mean she hasn't come home? Where is she?"

"I don't fucking know where she is."

"It was on the radio just now a girl was attacked in your street last night."

"Who was it? Did they give a name?"

"No, they didn't. And now you're telling me Sally is missing? I'm phoning the hospital."

"I already done that. She isn't there."

"I'm phoning the police then."

Just as she hung up the phone, the front door opened. Jagger looked out to the hall to see Sally standing there looking as rough as he did a few hours ago.

"Where the fuck have you been?"

"I went for a drink with them girls from last night."

"Till this time? What were you drinking? A full keg of beer?"

"No, we went to someone's house and I fell asleep."

"So you went with a bunch of strangers to a stranger's house, got shit-face drunk and fell asleep?"

"It wasn't like that."

"Pretty sure it was, Sally."

"Well, I'm home now."

"I've been up all fucking night worrying about you and you were at a party having a fucking ball."

"I'm sorry."

"You know what was the hardest bit of last night, Sally?"

"No. What?"

"It was after 3 a.m. when I knew all the pubs and clubs were shut. That whatever had happened whether you had been killed, raped or just away with another guy, the answer wasn't going to be good."

"I wasn't with another guy."

"Was it a girls' night this party then?"

"No, there was guys at it."

"And did you talk to them?"

"Yes, but you talk to girls all the time in the pub, Jagger."

"No, I sit with them while Ringo does the talking. Sally, for fuck's sake, I have been sitting thinking what has happened to you then your fucking mum phones saying a girl was attacked in our street last night."

"Who was it?"

"I don't fucking know, Sally, but right now it looks like I don't know much."

"What's that supposed to mean?"

"I don't know. I need to walk away right now before I say something I regret."

"Walk away or run away, Jagger?"

"No. Walk, Sally. I don't run from anything."

"It's all right. Stay where you are. I need to go and see my mum. She will be worried sick about all this."

Sally got some of her stuff together and walked out the flat, leaving Jagger sitting alone. In their flat it felt cold and empty. He sat there trying to work out how so much could change in just one night.

CHAPTER 6

STEALING HEARTS AND CASH...

That day Jagger went to work with a bad hangover and a broken heart. It did cross his mind to phone in sick but he was already on thin ice with his boss and being at work would keep him busy. A lot of people, even his pals, could never work out why the fuck Jagger wanted to work in the first place, never mind getting paid to work in a pot wash. But for Jagger it was ideal. He was born with asthma so he could never work in a factory with all the dust or on some building site in the cold weather. No, for him, this was perfect. He was inside, it was clean and warm and full of steam from the hot water, and they gave him food for free. He didn't need to worry about taking a fucking flask of tea and sandwiches.

No, he got breakfast, lunch and dinner all put down to him. But this shift was killing him. He wasn't hungry and every song on the radio made him think of Sally. He was needing a beer and a pal.

Later that day Ringo was sitting having a beer waiting for his pals when a guy with a black eye and a cut on his noise sat down at the table beside Ringo.

"You all right, mate?"

"Aye, I'm good, pal."

"You out for the day or you just out for a few?"

"No' sure yet, pal. Maybe the day. Who knows?"

"I've had a cunt of a day."

"Aye, looks like it."

"What do they call you?"

"Ringo, mate."

"Ringo? You a Beatles fan?"

"Love the Beatles, mate."

"They're all right. I wouldn't say they are the best but…"

"Easy, friend. That's my band you're talking about."

"So fucking what? What you going to do about it?"

"Look, pal, I know you're having a bad day but don't think you can take it out on me, ok?"

"Chill, wee man, it's all good."

Jagger and Syd walked in at the bar and the barmaid told them that the strange guy was looking for trouble. Jagger and Syd walked over and they didn't say a word to Ringo or each other. They both sat at different tables so the stranger thought they were all strangers.

"Look, wee man, I have been on it for days. I was just wanting to chat."

"That's cool, mate, but I'm no' up for talking much."

"Your mummy tell you no' to talk to strangers?"

"Aye, something like that."

"Buy us a pint, mate."

"Buy your own pint."

"Come on, wee man. Just a beer for fuck's sake."

Jagger stepped in. "Away and buy your own fucking beer."

"Who asked you?"

"No cunt but I'm telling you away and buy your own and while you're at the bar Ringo here and his two pals will take a beer."

"It's like that, is it?"

"Aye, it fucking is."

"You want a sore face, big man?"

"Why? You giving yours away?"

"Funny cunt."

"No, mate. I'm no' funny. I just don't like cunts like you who pick their victims."

"Look, lads—"

"Look fuck all. You came in here thinking you were a fucking vampire and my pal was the victim. But now you know you're the victim and you're surround by a pack of

115

vampires. Now, go and buy the beers of you will get fucking done in."

The guy went and got the beers and sat back down. "Look, lads. Is there any way I can walk out of here?"

Syd sat down beside him and pulled out a coin. "Right, cunt, this is how it's going to go. I will toss this coin and if it's heads we will kick your cunt in round the back of the pub."

"And what if it's tails?"

"You get another go."

"Fuck's sake, boys. I'm sorry."

"Get your smelly arse out of our pub and don't come back."

The guy got up and walked fast out the door. The boys all sat down at the one table to enjoy their free beers.

Ringo said, "They're called a coven or a clan."

"What are?"

"Vampires. They are no' known as a pack. It's a clan."

"Aye, all right, lost boy."

"Just saying, mate."

"How did the rest of date night go then?"

"Don't ask."

"Why? What's up?"

"She didn't come home till this morning. She went out drinking with them birds yous met in here last night."

"No big deal, mate."

"It is a big deal. My girlfriend stayed out all night. How's that no' a big deal?"

"Well, we have all been to a party. Time goes by fast."

"It's no' just that. It's been no' right for a while now. She is in a good job and I'm washing pot and pans. I think she's ashamed of me as her boyfriend."

"Don't be daft. She loves you."

"I know but she is moving on in life and I'm still sitting here with yous two."

"Thanks."

"Never mind. A few pints with your pals always helps."

"True."

"I know you're having a shit day, Jagger, but it's no' going to get any better in here."

"Why no'?"

"'Cause Del the Smell has just walked in."

"Is fat Ammo with him?"

"No."

"Good."

"All right, lads. Can I get a wee bit of hash please?"

"Sure, Del. Meet me in the toilets."

"I hate that smelly fat cunt."

"I know you do but he buys a lot of smoke from us."

"Where the fuck do cunts like him get the money when they don't do fuck all?"

"Fuck knows, mate."

Ringo came back to the table. "Looks like we are getting even more free beer."

"How?"

"Del has back money. He is getting the beers in."

"You should have told him no, Ringo."

"Fuck that. Free beer is free beer, mate. Even if it is from a smelly cunt."

Del came over with the pints. "Here you go, lads. Anything else?"

"Yeah. Do they sell cans of Lynx deodorant at the bar?"

"What?"

"Never mind Jagger. He is just being funny, Del."

"All right. Well, cheers, boys."

"Where or why did you get back money, Del?"

"I put a claim in last year but didn't hear back from them. So, I was thinking it was fucked but today the postman pops a cheque through my door. I was like, 'Well, happy days.'"

"You know it's cunts like you that is what's wrong with this fucking country, Del."

"Why is it?"

"Yous lazy arse cunts sit about doing fuck all and you think you should get a helping hand."

"Your two pals don't work."

"Aye, but they don't try and claim for extra money and they go out and deal a bit here and there to make a living."

"I do my bit too."

"Like what, Del?"

"I look after my mum, do her shopping and that."

"You're supposed to look after your mum. It's called being a fucking son but you look after her so you get extra money."

"No, it's no' like that."

"It's cunts like you who sit about all day spending hard working cunts' tax money and then you see the hard workers going away on holiday or something and you think that's no' fair I want a holiday."

"I've no' been on holiday for years."

"Have you no', mate? Well, go and get a fucking job like every cunt else and then you can go on one. Now fuck off, Del."

"Sorry, Jagger. Fuck's sake, man. I was only wanting to have a beer."

"Away to the bar and have one then."

"Ok. Bye, mate."

"You were a wee bit hard on him there, Jagger."

"Fuck him, Syd. He has been asking for it for a long time."

"I know but he is a good buyer, mate."

"He is a useless cunt. He couldn't pour piss out of a boot with the instructions written under the fucking heel."

"That's true, mate. Fuck him. He can go and buy hash elsewhere."

"Thanks, Ringo."

"It's ok to be a wee bit down, mate."

"My head is up my fucking arse."

"Broken heart sucks, man."

"You would know, Ringo."

"I would, lads. You know the worst thing about it?"

"No. What?"

"You end up missing them longer than you were with them."

"That's deep, Ringo."

"It's fucking true, lads. My cousin Bobby Bus Stop went off his head with a broken heart."

"Why did he get called Bobby Bus Stop?"

"Because he got knocked down with a bus."

"Fuck off."

"No, really. Anyway, he went nuts when his bird fucked off. He was going down to the bookies to put a line on a horse but he would write out the betting slip but never had any money to put it on."

"So what would he do?"

"Nothing. He would write out the slip and then just stand and watch the race and talk to himself."

"And what happened to him?"

"He lost it one day in the betting shop. He wrote out a betting slip for fifty pounds on a one-hundred-to-one horse and it fucking won."

"Poor bastard."

"I know. He got took away in a straitjacket and we didn't see him for years after that."

"How is he now?"

"Ok, but we have to keep an eye on him when it's the Grand National."

Syd handed Ringo a VHS video tape. "Here, Ringo. I have something for you."

"What film is it, Syd?"

"It's the porno I got hold of. It's good."

"Has it been keeping you company since Daisy fucked off?"

"We haven't spilt. We are just taking some time apart."

"Sure, mate. Here. Jagger will need this before me."

"I knew you were going to say that, Ringo."

"No, but you can have it first, mate. Watch it tonight and I will get it off you tomorrow."

"Smashing. Thanks, Ringo."

"Hope it's good, Syd. I'm a bit funny when it comes to porn."

"How? Do you only like gay porn?"

"No. Just some of it is shit. I like auntie porn."

"What's that? Like cunts who are against porn?"

"No. Auntie, like fucking your auntie."

"You are one sick cunt, Ringo."

"I'm sure a lot of guys like it. I mean, everyone had a hard-on when they seen their aunt in a night dress."

"Have you seen my auntie for fuck's sake?"

"Well, maybe no' yours but my aunt isn't much older than me, only by about six years, so when I was a wee guy at my gran's I would see her getting out the bath."

"Don't say it, Ringo."

"And I would sometimes get a Diego Maradona. There, I said it and I'm no' ashamed."

"You fucking should be."

"I need a drink."

"Another beer, Syd?"

"No. Whisky after all that."

"Aye. Jack and Coke for me. Help keep the wolf from the door."

"I will get them, boys."

"That was too much."

"He knows how to make us laugh, mate."

"True, Syd, but he also knows how to put the fear into us too."

A few hours and Jack Daniels later, Ringo told the boys, "You know, I was thinking about giving up the fags. I'm fed up with smoking and coughing my lungs up every morning."

"Aye, it's no' good, mate."

"They say it's hard getting off the smokes."

"My old man was off them for four years."

"Ringo, your old man was off them because he was in the jail and your mum wouldn't send him any money."

"Aye. She was keeping it for the bingo."

"Did she ever say, 'Ringo, I'm away to the bingo.'?"

"What's your weakness, Syd?"

"What do you mean?"

"Well, everyone has a weakness. With Ringo, it's smoking. So what's your weakness, mate?"

"No' sure."

"Is it whisky, beer, drugs or food?"

"Don't know. What about you?"

"Me? Well, that's easy. It's Jack Daniels."

"Whisky is your weakness."

"Aye. Jack has got me through some dark nights, I'm telling you."

"Well, whisky has got most cunts through some hard times. That's why they are all in here."

"Aye, let's face it, they are no' in for the Irn-Bru."

"Why Jack Daniels, Jagger? Is it because Keith Richards drinks it?"

"Aye, maybe was at first but now it's all different reasons. Like when I open a bottle I always say to Sally, 'It smells like Christmas.'"

"Why Christmas?"

"Back in the day when I didn't have much money that was the only time I could afford it. So now when I smell it I always think of Christmas."

"You have drank a good bit over the years, mate."

"Aye. Al Pacino calls it John Daniels in *Scent of a Woman*."

"Why does he call it John?"

"He says, 'If you have known him as long as I have, you get to call him John.'"

"I remember you were the only cunt in here who drank it. Everyone else was still drinking Bells."

"Aye. Even way back then Cagney and Lacey would say, 'You only drink this because of Keith Richards.'"

"What the fuck would they know?"

"You know the best Keith Richards story I ever read? It was the blind angel."

"What's the blind angel?"

"Well, in the late seventies, the Stones were on tour in Canada. They were playing three nights in a row at the venue. So the first night some of the road crew come to the Stones and tell them this blind girl has turned up alone and she is right at the front. They are amazed that she hasn't just showed but she got there early to get down at the front. So Keith tells them at the end of the show, 'Take her home in my limo. I don't want her trying to get home alone.'"

"That was nice of him."

"Yeah, but then on the second night she shows up again down at the front alone. So Keith tells the crew same again: 'Get her my limo and get her home.' And again the third night she is there and they look after her. Keith tells them, 'Make sure she gets my ride and home safe.' So a few weeks later the Stones are back in Canada and Keith gets busted for having heroin in his hotel room. They take him to jail and the rest of the Stones have to leave him in Canada.

"Did he do time?"

"Well, because it was heroin he was looking at doing twelve years. He was fucked. It was the end of the Stones and the end of him."

"So, what happened?"

"Well, one day, the judge who was to decide what to do with this drug addict rock star was sitting at home when his daughter's friend showed up and she asked to speak to her friend's dad. The judge sat down with his daughter's blind best friend and the girl told him the story about how she went alone three nights in a row to the Rolling Stones gigs and how this rock star went out of his way to help her."

"The blind bird was the daughter's friend?"

"Yeah, and after that the judge decided to let him off as long as he went to rehab and the Stones done a gig in Canada and all the money from that night went to a charity for the blind."

"And is that why he calls her his blind angel?"

"Yeah."

"And did the Stones do the gig?"

"Aye, and story goes that a guy bumped into Bill Wyman backstage and he said, 'Watch where you are going. Are you blind or something?'"

"No way."

"The rest of the band had to tell him that most of the people backstage were."

"That's put me in the mood for a Jack Daniels. What about you, Ringo?"

"Put me in the mood for some brown sugar, Syd."

"Wait, Syd, you still haven't told us your weakness."

"No' sure, lads. I think just now it's Daisy. I can't live without her. As far as I'm concerned she is my moon in a dark night."

"Well, let's hope to fuck she feels the same about you or you're going to find yourself on the fucking dark side of the moon."

"Hate to say it but Ringo is right. I mean, just look around you. The pub is filled with lost souls."

"Aye or we as like to call them the 'my baby left me' gang."

"You must feel the same way about Sally, Jagger."

"I do, mate, but all I'm saying is some guys can't deal with a broken heart. They can be the best fighters you have ever seen and scared from no cunt but when it comes to love it cuts them down and they run away a hide in the pub."

"Aye, hiding in the shadows. Syd, don't let that be you."

"I won't, Ringo. Don't worry."

"Got to be like me. One night is plenty."

"I think with Sally the problem is I gave her my heart but she wanted my soul."

"Ok, no more Jack Daniels for fucking Bob Dylan over here."

"No, the night is young."

"You need to be like a flamingo, Syd, and put your foot down."

"Funny, Ringo."

"Look, lads, I know it's no' your scene but we can make good money if we rob a shop or something like that."

"I'm no' into that, Ringo."

"I'm out too, mate."

"Look, lads. It's easy. No cunt will know apart from us. I have a few places lined up. In and out, no cunt gets hurt and we get rich."

"I knew you had been back on the rob. You have been spending like a drunken sailor."

"Look, we can pop out of here and be back within the hour. No one will notice that we are gone."

"I'm no' sure. What do you think, Jagger?"

"How much could we make?"

"About anything up to a grand."

"No' worth it for a grand, Ringo."

"Look, you want big money in one go? That's when the cops come looking for you, so you keep it low. A few bucks here, a few bucks there. Easy. Like under the radar and all that."

"Where you thinking of next?"

"The chip shop."

"Fuck that. There is no money in the fucking chip shop, Ringo."

"Think how many lazy fat cunts go to the chip shop every night."

"He's right, Jagger. It's always busy."

"Aye, if it's busy then we can't do it."

"It won't always be busy the whole night. We go in, tell them what we want and back out into the dark night, back to the pub, get a drink and talk to a few cunts so they remember we were in here. Job done."

"What was the last thing you robbed?"

"A bus at the end of the night for a bag of coins. About three hundred pounds in it and no cunt came looking."

"I'm still no' sure."

"It will be fun. We can have a Jack D and a wee line of coke and head off. We will be back here in no time. Don't worry so much, lads. I will go and get us some masks for our faces. We will look the part. Trust me."

"And what about weapons? We can't just run in with our dicks in our hands now, can we?"

"Don't worry about that, Jagger. I'm on it, mate. Back soon, boys. Don't move."

Ringo ran out the pub leaving a very drunk Jagger and Syd speechless looking at each other.

"What you thinking, Jagger?"

"I will tell you what I'm thinking. Our pal is going to end up in the jail if he keeps this up."

"So we are no' doing it?"

"No, Syd. I'm out, mate."

"If you're out, then I'm out but you can tell him."

"Cool. I will tell him to chill the fuck out."

"He is making good money by the sounds of it."

"Aye, but the cops will already be looking. They are no' daft."

"Aye. No doubt we will end up with undercover cops sitting in here again. Don't look round but our pal has just walked in with his gang of bums."

"Who? The Crow?"

"Yep."

"Great."

"How has he been with you since all that shit?"

"He has been fine. As good as you could ask from him. Because he is and always will be a cunt."

"All right, Jagger. All right, Syd," said the Crow. "Where's your wee pal Ringo? He no' out tonight?"

"He's kicking about here somewhere, mate."

"You needing any hash, Syd? The boys have got some good stuff at a good price for you."

"What? Mates rates?"

"Always, Syd. Anything for a pal."

"I will get Ringo in a minute. See what we need."

"What about you, Jagger?"

"What about me?"

"You needing anything?"

"No, I'm good, thanks."

"You sure? Maybe something to help you sleep in your empty bed, mate?"

"What the fuck do you mean by that?"

"Nothing, Jagger. Just people talk and the word is you're out the big bed, mate."

"Do you ever take a day off from being a fucking nightmare?"

"I'm just saying what everyone is saying."

"And what's that?"

"That Sally has left you and she is busy with her work friends in the toon."

"That's bullshit."

"So does she still love you then?"

"Has anyone ever loved you?"

"Jesus, mate."

"Jesus might love you but I think you're a cunt."

"Listen, Jagger, this is the second time I have had to tell you to watch your mouth, son. There won't be a third time, ok?"

Just as the Crow was walking back to the bar, Ringo walked in with his sports bag full of his robbing gear.

"All right, Ringo. What the fuck you up to?"

"Nothing much, Crow."

"I told Syd I have some smoke for you."

"Cool. I will get some in a minute." Ringo walked over to his friends. "Ok, what the fuck did I miss?"

"Nothing much. Just Jagger and the Crow going head to head again."

"Fucking hell, mate. Let it go with him."

"It was him who was at it. Talking about Sally. The cunt."

"It won't end well with him."

"Ringo, this chip shop thing is a bad idea, mate."

"Why?"

"It just is. Nothing good will come of it."

"We could make a bit of money tonight, Jagger."

"Look, mate, I don't have the time or the crayons to explain this to you. It's no' going to happen. End of."

"Ok, let's get the drinks in and enjoy our night."

Syd walked back over having just had a line of coke. He handed the small bag of white powder to Ringo just as a young good looking girl walked over to the table.

"Hi, Jagger," she said as Ringo and Syd sat side by side looking the young good looking girl up and down.

"Hi, Angela. How's you?"

"I'm good, Jagger, thanks. You want a drink?"

"No, thanks. My pal just got me one."

"Is this your pals?"

Jagger thought, *Fucking hell no. I don't need this.* "Aye. This is Ringo and Syd."

"Hello, boys."

"Lads, this is Angela from work."

"Hi, Angela from work."

"Nice to meet you, hen."

"You too. I'm just going to get my drink from my pal. I will be back in a wee minute."

"Well, well… Jagger has a work friend."

"Fuck up, Ringo."

"She is a no' bad wee bit of stuff, mate."

"She is just a girl I know from work."

"You never told us you had work friends."

"Aye. That's how it is in the real world, lads. When you go out and work you meet new people."

"Ok. Don't get angry. You will upset Angela."

"Look, don't say fuck all about what we do in here and don't offer her a line of coke, Ringo."

Angela came back over to the table. "So, boys, what you up to tonight? Staying here or going into town?"

"We stay here. We don't like the toon, hen."

"Yeah, we just like to have a few beers here."

"Cool, so how does a girl get a line in here?"

"Here you go, hen. Have some of mine." Ringo gave her the bag of powder as Jagger looked on very unhappy.

As she walked to the toilet Jagger grabbed Ringo. "What the fuck did I say?"

"What? She fucking asked for some. She is no' daft."

"You could have said, 'No, hen. We don't touch the stuff.'"

"She knows. Ask Syd."

"Aye, she is no' daft. She knows we are on it tonight and anyway looks like she has her eye on you."

"Who, me?"

"No, you, Ringo. Fuck's sake. On Jagger."

"I don't need this. No' tonight."

"What's wrong? You are only having a drink with a girl from work."

"Yeah, no worse than Sally out all night with strangers, is it?"

"Shut up, Ringo. You know, Ringo, sometimes I envy cunts that don't know you, mate."

"What did I say wrong?"

Angela came back from the toilet and gave Ringo his wee bag of powder back. "Thanks, Ringo. That's good stuff."

"Any time, hen."

"My pals won't come over here. One of them says yous are bad news."

Jagger laughed.

"Who is? Hell no. We are the good guys in here. So, Angela, how long you been work friends with Jagger?"

"A wee while, no?"

"Do you both work in the pot wash. I hear it's very hot and steamy in there."

"Yeah, I go in when it's busy and help Jagger out."

"You help him out, really?"

"Shut up, Ringo, my soon to be old friend."

"I'm just getting to know Angela."

"Why don't you and Syd go to the bar and get a round in?"

"It's really good to see you out of work, Jagger."

"And you, Angela. I hope you have a good night out with your pals. No, wait, your pals are having a shit night because Ringo is talking to them."

"They will be fine. They can handle Ringo and Syd. Don't worry."

"I just hope they don't offer your pals drugs, that's all."

"What? My pals will take them. That's why we came in here. Well, and to see if you were in."

"And I'm here but I'm always in here."

"Good to know, Jagger."

As Jagger and Angela sat talking waiting for the boys to come back from the bar Sally went to walk in the door of the pub. As she put her hand on the door she looked through the door window and saw Jagger and a young pretty girl drinking and laughing. She was frozen. She couldn't move. She just stood there in the cold night looking into the warm pub where the love of her life looked like he was on a date and moving on fine without her. She turned away from the pub and walked away into the cold dark night.

The next morning Jagger woke up naked on the floor of his flat. His head was banging, he felt sick and he could only open one eye. *What the fuck happened last night? How the fuck did I end up here?*

He stood up in the nude looking around his flat with still just one eye open. "Hello? Any my pals here?"

He remembered the girl from last night and thought, *Shit.* "Anybody here? Male or female?"

No answer. He was all alone.

He headed into the kitchen to get a drink of water and look for some painkillers. *What the fuck was I drinking last night?* He felt weak and dizzy standing drinking water out the kitchen tap. His house phone started ringing and he walked into the next room but everything was in his way because he still only had one eye open.

"Hello?"

"Jagger, you ok?"

"Aye, who is it?"

"It's Syd, mate. Where did you go to last night?"

"No' sure, Syd. Just woke up in here naked like the fucking American werewolf of Glasgow. I have a cunt of a sore head, mate."

"Same here. It's banging."

"I feel like I need put down I'm that ill."

"It was a fun night so worth it."

"Syd, what happened to that bird Angela? Please tell me nothing happened."

"No, mate. She left with her pals but told you to phone her."

"Thank fuck for that. I had the fear there."

"Do you have the bag, Jagger?"

"What bag?"

"The bag from last night."

"I'm no' sure, mate. I don't know what the fuck you are on about and I don't know where my clothing or my girlfriend is, mate. I'm standing here naked. I have fuck all."

"If you don't have the bag then Ringo must have it."

"No, wait, it's here… the sports bag. Hey, thank fuck we didn't do what that mad cunt was wanting to do."

Jagger opened the bag and looked in, still with just one eye open, and pulled out money. Ten-pound notes, five-pound notes and bags of coins.

"Syd, I have the fear again. Please tell me we didn't."

"Aye, we did, Jagger, and how's your eye?"

"It won't fucking open. What happened to my eye, Syd?"

"Well, it happened in the chip shop. Look, maybe we shouldn't be talking on the phone. Mate, I will head over later."

"No, Syd, you and Ringo head over now, mate."

"I can't. I'm going to meet Daisy for a drink. Try and work things out. I will head over after, mate."

Jagger hung the phone up and got a flashback from last night. It was all a blur he remembered having a mask and pulling it down a bit to take some coke. They were out in the street. Syd was saying he wasn't sure about this and Jagger and Ringo were laughing at him telling him to take a bit of coke and go. He remembered women shouting at him and another outside in the street calling them dirty fucking bastards.

His house phone rang again and Jagger picked it up. "Hello?"

"Jagger, it's Syd again."

"Why you phoning me, Syd? You should be on your way here, mate."

"We have a problem. It's Ringo."

"What the fuck is it?"

"He must've fallen asleep in the pub toilets last night. He has been locked in the pub all fucking night."

"Where the fuck is he just now, Syd?"

"Down at the pub with the cops and Cagney and Lacey."

"Fucking hell. Why are the cops there? He's just a drunk guy in a pub."

"The cleaner found him passed out on the bar. He has been drinking most of the night in the pub. Maybe Cagney and Lacey want him to pay up for what he drank. I don't know for sure."

"Look, Syd, you go down there and get fucking John McClane and bring him here."

"Ok, mate. Don't worry. I'll talk to the cops and tell them he will pay for the drink and it will all be fine."

"Smashing, Syd. See you soon."

An hour or two went by but it felt like a week for Jagger. He decided to get out his emergency bag of coke and he poured himself a large Jack Daniels and ice and took two Valium to take the edge off his fear.

He sat waiting for his two pals to show up. He sat waiting and thinking how everything was falling apart in his life. He hadn't seen or heard from Sally and felt like without her his life would go down the wrong path. He knew he needed to pick up the phone and call her but he couldn't just now. He needed to make sure all this shit from last night got worked out first then he would call her. If she only knew that every night since she left to go back to her mum's that Jagger had sat alone by the phone drinking and waiting for her to call. Night after night but it would never ring as if she had vanished like a dream and left Jagger in a nightmare he couldn't wake up from.

Syd walked in. "You ok, Jagger?"

"No, mate, I'm pretty far from ok."

"You look like shit."

"Thanks. Where the fuck is John fucking *Die Hard*?"

"He is away to get Cagney and Lacey the money he owes them for the booze he drank last night."

"What the fuck happened?"

"No' sure. He must've passed out in the toilets and they didn't check them and he woke up about three in the morning. And he didn't think about getting out or getting help or calling anyone, he just sat at the bar drinking."

"Well, aye, free bar is what he would have been thinking."

"So, he drank till he passed out again and then the poor cleaner found him. Aye, face down on the bar with a bottle of whisky beside him."

"He is a fucking nightmare that boy, I'm telling you."

"Well, by the looks of it you're no' any better sitting here with a bag of coke and a whisky looking like Scarface."

"Talking about Scarface, what happened to my eye?"

"What, you don't remember?"

"No, Syd, I don't."

"It happened in the chip shop. You and Ringo ran in and I stood at the door keeping watch but the old dear in the shop was hard as nails, mate. She wasn't for handing over fuck all and as Ringo was shouting at her, she grabbed the handle for the basket which was sitting in the hot fat and she throws it at you and Ringo. But Ringo got out of the way of it."

"And it got me."

"Aye, mate. A big single black pudding came flying off it and hit you bang on the eye, mate."

"My eye is fucking killing me now."

"It was killing you as soon as it happened. You slid down the wall screaming, 'Jesus suffering fuck, my fucking eye,' and the old dear was saying, 'That's what you fucking get.'"

"Did anyone else see us?"

"Just some old lady outside shouting about getting her man's tea."

"So the cops will be on the lookout for some cunt with a sore eye?"

"Yeah. Maybe you should keep your head down for a bit, mate."

Ringo walked in out of breath. "All right, boys. Here, Jagger, do me a line and I will have a whisky too, thanks."

"Get a glass and get Syd a beer."

"I have a bit of bad news, mate."

"I know, Ringo. The cops are looking for some cunt who looks like one-eyed Jack."

"Well, yeah. Maybe you should get out the way for a bit, mate."

"I will need to now."

Ringo held his belly in pain.

"You ok, mate?"

"My belly is killing me, lads?"

"It will be the way You have been sleeping on that bar all night."

"I'm no' sure, lads I've had it a while now."

"It might be cancer, Ringo."

Ringo stuttered. "Is cancer s-s-sore, lads?"

"No, but it does give you a cunt of a stutter, mate."

"Funny cunt."

"Right, this is the plan. I'm going to get away for a bit. Go to a wee hotel up north and let my eye heal."

"Cool. And me and Ringo will keep an eye out. You get it? Keep an eye out… Aye, anyway, we will see if the cops are hanging about."

"Aye, maybe this is a good thing. I can ask Sally to come with me."

"Wait, that's the news I had to tell you, Jagger. Sally was out in the toon with a guy last night."

"What fucking guy?"

"No' sure. It was some cunt who buys hash from us. Told me this morning he seen her last night. Might be nothing. Just a work mate."

"Or she has moved on and I'm sitting waiting for her to come back like a cunt."

"Only way to find out is to call her."

"I can't just now."

"Well, it looks like one of us is going up north with you then."

"Smashing."

CHAPTER 7

HIDING IN THE SHADOWS...

The next morning Jagger was at the train station sitting waiting to see which one of his pals was going with him. The day before they were not sure who could go and who would stay and sell a bit of hash and hang about the pub like normal and try to find out if anyone was talking about the chip shop getting robbed.

As Jagger sat there watching loved ones saying goodbye to each other, he couldn't help but think about Sally. It didn't matter where he was or what he was doing, she was always in his head. Jagger saw the train from Penilee pull in. He waited, looking to see who had showed up. He hoped it was Syd. Not that he didn't want it to be Ringo. It was just he wanted a few quiet days and he would get it with Syd and Syd was going through his own shit with Daisy so he would be wanting some time away to think. Aye, he was sure it would be his old pal Syd, who would let him have a chilled few days.

"All right, Jagger. You want anything from the shop?"

Fuck, it was Ringo. "No, thanks, mate."

"What?"

"I said no, thanks."

"I'm going to get us a few cans."

Ringo walked up with his bag of cans. Jagger met him outside the shop.

"All right, Jagger. What time is the train?"

"We have plenty of time, Ringo. Let's get something to eat in McDonald's."

As they sat in McDonald's having a bit of food, Ringo didn't look happy.

"You all right, mate?"

"Aye, I'm just no' too keen on McDonald's, you know."

"I know, mate, but it gets something in our belly, Ringo."

"Aye, I know. It's just always busy as fuck, cunts banging into you... I feel like killing cunts in here."

"We are pretty much on the run, Ringo. Killing cunts is no' a good idea, mate."

"Look at all the mums and dads all fed up. They used to be just like us now they're all fucked, stuck with their wee brats crying all fucking day for a McDonald's."

"It happens to us all. We all get old. We all become our dads."

"Look at some of them but that poor guy over there he is no' much older than us and he is that fed up he is making his kids' Happy Meal sad."

"Aye, he will give up his whole life for them brats and at the end when he is done they will fuck him off into a home."

"That's no' happening to me. Fuck that. I'm going to live fast and die young."

"Well, can you stay alive for the next few days? Maybe just till my eye has healed? Then you can check out."

"For you? Sure. Let's have some fun."

"We are no' going away for fun. We are going to let the dust settle."

"I know but we can't sit about a room. We need to go out for food and beer."

"Cool, let's go. The train will be here soon."

Jagger and Ringo got a table on the train out the way of everyone.

"This will do," said Jagger.

"Jagger, I need to sit there."

"Why? What's up with that side of the table?"

"If I sit there I will be going backwards. I hate that feeling."

"Well, I don't like it either."

"Ok, we can both sit at this side then."

"Can we fuck, Ringo. We'll look like a fucking couple."

"So? Fuck, who cares? No cunts know us here."

"I care, mate."

"Maybe looking like a gay couple is good. After all, as you said, we are on the run."

"Look, you sit at this side. Fuck's sake. The train hasn't left the fucking station yet and you are doing my fucking nut in."

"Sorry. I have a hangover, mate. A few beers and I will be sound."

"Maybe you need a rub doon with a deed doo."

"Who says that again?"

"Old Mick in the pub."

"So he does. Any time he gets his first pint, I say, 'You ok, Mick?' and he always says that."

"Aye. He is a good old cunt and strong as fuck too. One night some cunt was trying to take the piss out of him and Mick went for the guy, and me and Syd grabbed hold of him and he was a strong guy."

"Aye, because he works six days a week and has a drink every day and never up or down."

"That's because guys like Mick drink beer."

"I drink beer every day."

"No, Ringo, you drink lager every day."

"What's the difference?"

"Well, old Mick has drank nothing but beer and wine all his days. You know, Eldorado wine and beer. I mean, ale, no' lager. It's a lot better for you than what we drink."

"So, what you're saying is if I drink beer and wine and no lager and whisky I will live longer?"

"Who knows, mate, you might."

"No' a bad way to look at it."

"But you just said about an hour ago you were going to die young so just stick with the whisky."

"No, but it is a good way to look at it. I mean, I drink lager, you drink beer, we both get drunk but you get an extra few years to live."

"Aye. I might get an extra year or two but it will be an extra year of being an old cunt stinking of piss and never getting my hole."

"Your no' getting your hole just now."

"That's my choice, dickhead."

The boys decided to get off the train and get the ferry to Millport. They jumped a wee bus into the main part of the island and Jagger went to the B&B to check them in. Ringo headed to the shop to buy smokes.

Jagger walked into an old lovely wee B&B. The reception had an old open fire and Jagger thought, *This will do.*

"Good afternoon, how can I help?"

"Hi there. I would like a room for me and my pal for a few nights, thanks."

"How many nights?"

"I'm no' sure. Three or four maybe."

"Then why did you say a few nights? A few means two."

"Ok, what would I say for four then?"

"Well, four is four."

"Well, four it is then. Aye, four nights, cheers."

"And did you say your friend as well?"

"Aye, my pal, that's right."

"And where is your pal."

"He's away to get some fags."

"Some what?"

"Some smokes."

"Ok, would you like breakfast?"

"No, thanks. I'm looking for a bit of lunch now, mate."

"No, sir. I mean, would you like breakfast in the morning?"

"No, we'll still probably be in our kips, mate."

"Very good. We lock the main door at midnight but there's a night watchman who will let you in. And don't be too drunk if you go to the pub."

"No, just a few beers for us."

"My daughter will show you to the room. This is Heather."

"Hi, Heather."

"Hello. What room you in?"

"No' sure. Your dad didn't say."

"It will be on the key ring."

"Right. Aye, it's room 27, pal. Thanks."

"What you here for?"

"Just a few days away with my mate, you know."

"Aye. Here to get drunk?"

"Aye, but don't tell your old man."

"Don't worry about him. He has been in a bad mood since my mum left him."

"Right and I was sure he was suffering from TMB."

"What's that?"

"Too many birthdays."

"I think he is. Anyway, this is you. I hope you and your friend have fun."

"He is no' my boyfriend."

"What?"

"I'm just saying… he is no' my boyfriend because it could look like that, you know. Two gays, I mean, guys getting away for a few nights."

"Four nights… you must really love him?"

"What? No, we're just two old pals."

"I'm just joking."

"Ok, cool. Thanks, Heather. I'm Jagger."

"Cool name. See you later, Jagger."

Jagger met Ringo outside the B&B and they walked into the local pub just down the road to get a pint. As they ordered a beer at the bar, Jagger looked around the pub. It looked friendly and had an old open fire too.

"Looks no' bad in here, Ringo."

"Aye, looks all right, mate. Them two guys standing at the other side of the bar…"

"Yeah, what about them?"

"Do you think they are the local drug dealers?"

"No, I don't, mate. They are just two guys out for a pint."

"Money lenders then."

"No, Ringo. They are two local guys or two cunts on holiday like us."

"On holiday to Millport… that's sad."

"What's sad about it? A lot of people go on holiday here. Everyone loves Scotland."

"Spain is better."

"You just want the sun, mate."

"Makes you feel good and it's better than here stuck in the rain on the run."

"You just going to tell everyone in the bar? Shut it."

"There's a Chinese down the road. You want something to eat?"

"Aye, soon. After a few beers, maybe."

"I had a look at the menu. It looks good."

"Aye? What they got?"

"Everything from a spring roll to hell if I know."

"That's good."

"Aye."

Jagger heard the two guys at the end of the bar had English accents and they were making fun of a wee guy sitting alone by the fire having a pint.

"You hear them, Ringo?"

"Hear who?"

"The guys making fun of that wee guy by the fire."

"No. What did they say?"

"No' sure. I think the wee guy is a local and the two cunts are English."

"And they think they can take the piss out of the wee guy?"

"Aye, they do."

"We can't be having that. Us Scots need to stick together when it comes to the English."

"All right, chill, William Wallace. Remember we are trying to keep our heads down."

"Ok, but if they keep it up…"

"I know. We will deal with them."

A tall young blonde girl walked into the pub and ordered a drink at the bar.

"Fucking hell, Ringo. Check out the big blonde honey."

"Well, shag my dick. I'm in love."

"Aye. I think we need to take a seat so we can hide our erections."

"She is stunning, Jagger."

"She is no' bad. I bet everyone on this island is in love with her."

"Picture this, Jagger. Me and her back at the B&B, black bra, black thong, hold ups and high heels."

"Aye, sounds good."

"Aye, but fuck knows what she would be wearing, mate."

Just as they were looking at the hot blonde, Jagger heard the two guys at it again with the wee local guy by the fire.

"Hey, son, you old enough to be drinking in here?"

The wee guy just kept drinking his pints.

"You not got homework tonight?" they laughed.

"Leave the guy alone," Jagger said.

"Sorry, mate?"

"I said leave the guy alone. Did you no' hear me?"

"Look, my friend, we were just having a laugh. No harm done."

Ringo stepped in. "Aye, a good fucking laugh *at* him, no' *with* him. And we are no' your friends."

"Look, lads, we're sorry. We did think he was underage and you wouldn't get away with it down south."

"If he's big enough to hold a pint, then he's big enough to drink it, the bar man says."

"Ok, lads. Again, sorry. Let us buy you a beer."

"No, you're all right, pal. Maybe get the wee guy one."

As Jagger turned to talk to Ringo about it, he was gone. Jagger looked around the pub and there was Ringo talking to the blonde.

The bar man gave Jagger a pint. "Here, son. This is on me."

"Why?"

"For shutting them two fuckers up."

"No problem, mate. I didn't think it would be hard with my pal as back-up but he has fucked off over there."

"Don't worry, son. He will be back soon."

"How do you know that?"

"Well, he is no' her type."

"No?"

"No, son. Your pal is, let's just say, barking up the wrong tree."

As Jagger sat down at a table to enjoy his pint by the fire, Ringo came back over.

"How did you get on, mate?"

"Fucking no chance there, mate."

"Why? What's up?"

"What's up is she likes the fanny more than I do by the sounds of it."

"You heartbroken again, Ringo?"

"It's a waste of a good woman, that's what it is, mate."

"She is that, Ringo. She is stunning."

"You know what I don't get."

"Her fanny tonight by the sounds of it."

"No. What I don't get is if they don't like cock…"

"They as in lesbians? Aye, go on."

"If they don't like the cock then why do they like dildos?"

"I don't think it's the dick that's the problem with lesbians, mate. It's the cunt who is attached to it is the problem."

"Maybe we could get her and her girlfriend—"

"No. Hell no, Ringo."

"You don't know what I'm going to say."

"I have a good idea, mate."

"No, hear me out. Maybe we could have a drink with them and go back to the B&B and if they go for it we could watch."

"That will never happen. You watch too much porn, Ringo."

"Do you think there is a strip club here?"

"Aye, there is, mate."

"Where is it?"

"Well, you go out here, get the bus to the ferry, then get off the ferry and get the train at Largs to Glasgow and that gets you into the toon where you will find the strip club."

"This is going to be a long few days. No strip club and all the birds are lesbians."

"Can't you just look at it as a chilled few days away from the city?"

"Could do."

"We need to just have a beer and keep our heads down. It's no' a fucking Ibiza weekend."

"I know. It's just the people here are no' our people."

"I know that, but we don't need to talk to them."

"They look like the cunts who go to Disneyland and they don't have kids."

"Aye or the cunts when you were wee and went to the Christmas panto and you would see adults who didn't have kids with them."

"The cunts were there to steal kids."

"I went one year and we were on the first balcony and my arse hit my paper cup of Coke and it fell onto all the old aged pensioners below. They went nuts and I got put out on the bus with the driver while everyone else watched the show. I helped the driver with his crossword."

"I thought you were going to say you helped him with his cock."

"No, only thing that was hard was his crossword, thank fuck."

"That must've been a cunt of a day out."

"Even better. After that our summer school trip was to the Magnum centre to go swimming and as we were waiting to go in, we all got a slush and when I was looking away a guy in my year stuck a straw in my slush and drank most of it."

"What did you do?"

"I turned round and seen what he was doing, so I hit him right in the eye and that was me dragged out back on the bus with the driver again."

"Your old pal."

"Aye. When the teacher knocked on the bus door, the driver opened it and said, 'Just in time. I'm stuck on twelve across.'"

The next day the boys were asleep when they heard a chap at the door. Jagger looked through the peep hole.

"Who is it, Jagger?"

"It's the dickhead manager."

"Hello? I can hear you in there. Open the door please."

Jagger opened the door and the manager walked in looking at the mess of empty cans and takeaways all over the room.

"You boys had fun by the looks of it."

"We did, thanks."

"You here to tell us breakfast is ready?"

"No, breakfast is for guests who pay for breakfast and you didn't. No, I'm here to tell you if you are out drinking again tonight when you get in you have to keep it down. My other guests were not happy with you last night."

"No' our fault all of your guests go to bed at eight."

"It doesn't matter what time they go to bed, son."

"I'm no' your son."

"Yes, well, you need to keep it down or you will have to find somewhere else, ok?"

"Aye, cool, Basil. Whatever you say."

"Have a good day, boys."

"What a wanker, waking us up this early in the morning."

"Ringo, it's 2 p.m., mate."

"Well, I have a cunt of a hangover and I like to sleep though my hangovers."

"I know how you feel. My heed is banging. You want a can?"

"No, I want food and a pint and some painkillers."

"Ok, let's go. Ding ding, round two."

As the boys were about to head out the door they met Heather the manager's daughter.

"Afternoon, Jagger. What you up to today?"

"Just going for a beer."

"We have a bar here, you know."

"Aye, but we want some food too."

"I can make yous something. Is this your pal?"

"Aye, this is Ringo."

"Hi, Ringo."

"Hello. I didn't know there was a young good looking girl working here."

"Don't start. She is Basil Fawlty's daughter."

"I'm sorry to hear that."

"Hear what?"

"That your dad is your boss."

"Yeah, it's no' easy having your dad as a boss."

"I bet, hen. I only hope he is a better dad than he is a boss."

"Ringo, give it up, for fuck's sake."

"No, that's all right. I know my dad can be hard work but it is better just to let him get his own way."

"Keeps the peace, Heather."

"It does, Jagger. Anything for a quiet life."

"Maybe when you have finished your shift today, you could come out with us for a drink."

"I can't, but thanks for asking, Ringo."

"How no'?"

"I work all day, pretty much every day."

"That's no' right. You should get time off."

"I take it you working every day is down to your dad."

"Yes, Jagger. He says he can't afford to bring in anyone else."

"Your old man is a cunt, hen."

"Fuck's sake, Ringo."

"Well, he is."

"It's all right. I know my dad is old-fashioned."

"And a cunt."

"Yes, Ringo, and a cunt but it won't be forever."

"Look, Heather, I think what Ringo is trying to say is that every family has a cunt in it and the cunt in your family is your dad."

"Aye, and that's a good thing, hen."

"How's that, Ringo?"

"Because if you don't know who the cunt is in your family then it's probably you."

"Thank God I know it's my dad then."

"Best way to look at it, hen."

"I will go and see what I can make yous boys to eat."

"That's no' right, Jagger."

"What?"

"The way her old man has her working like a fucking slave all the time."

"You're right, mate, but I'm sure she will leave some day or he will do her a favour and fuck off and die."

"Maybe we could help her."

"No, Ringo, I'm no' going to tell you again. We are here to keep our heads down no' get involved in other people's shit."

"I know, Jagger, but maybe it's good karma helping the weak."

"No, Ringo, we are no' the fucking A Team, mate. Now let it go."

"Well, maybe she could come back to Glasgow with us."

"Aye, that's just what she needs. To leave this beautiful island and come and hang about fucking Glasgow."

"Right, boys, I can make you cheeseburgers and chips. How does that sound?"

"Sounds spot on, Heather. Thank you."

"Cool, ok. With the food and two beers, that will be, let's say, ten pounds."

"Cool, hen. Jagger will get it."

"Aye, as always, Jagger gets it."

"I'm sorry I have to charge you, but my dad will know I have made food for you so he will look at the bill later."

"It's cool, Heather. Don't worry. Here you go and get yourself a drink."

"Tell me, Heather. It's no' your dad who is making the food, is it?"

"No, don't worry, Ringo. I'm making it. My dad is, let's just say, always busy this time of day."

"Busy? Where?"

"You don't need a watch when you work with my dad. He has a time for everything and with it being three… Well, he is busy in the toilet."

"What? Every day at three he goes for a shit?"

"Yes, Ringo, every day. He even makes me clean the toilets at half past two so he knows they are clean for him at three."

Ringo sat looking at the gents door. "And how many cubicles are in there, Heather?"

"Two. Why?"

"No, nothing. Just thinking he is keeping you busy."

"Ok. Enjoy your beer. Your food won't be long."

"What you thinking, Ringo?"

"Me? Nothing, mate."

"I know that look."

"No, I'm just thinking he is an old cunt."

"Aye, well, fuck him. We will be away back to Glasgow in a day or two and will never have to see that old cunt again."

"Aye, but Heather will every fucking day and that's no' right."

"Look, she will be fine. He will probably leave this hotel to her."

"Never thought of that. Now she is getting better looking thinking about that."

"Leave her alone, Ringo. She already has a cunt in her life. She doesn't need another one."

"What is up with you today? You're doing more moaning than a French hooker."

"Maybe I'm fed up, mate."

"With what?"

"With the fact I'm on the run."

"You're no' on the fucking run. You have a sore eye and when it's better we will go home."

"It's better now. Fuck this."

"Ok, we will go home tomorrow. Just phone Syd and see if the cops are hanging about."

"For your sake they better no' be, mate."

"You need to chill out."

"And you need to buy a fucking round now and then."

"I have."

"I didn't see you jumping in to pay for the beer and food there."

"I will get the next round. No big deal."

"Aye, the next round when it's only two pints. I'm telling you, Ringo, you are as tight as a heterosexual's arsehole in an orgy."

"I'm fed up to fuck with you. I'm going to ask Heather to come out for a drink."

"When you taking her? On her lunch break? She told you her old man has her working night and day."

"Well, she needs a day off like every cunt. She needs to let off some steam."

"I know, mate. You're right and I'm sorry for being a cunt today."

"What, just today?"

"Aye. I'm just fed up. I hate waiting."

"Waiting for what?"

"Everything, Ringo. I hate waiting to find out if the cops are looking for us. I hate waiting for a bus. Or getting a tattoo. I mean, once I'm in the chair I'm good, let's go. But sitting in the shop waiting your turn is a fucking killer."

"What do you hate waiting for the most, Jagger?"

"For the day Sally tells me it's over."

"You think it's coming?"

"Aye, it's in the post, Ringo, but knowing my luck it's coming second class so I will have to fucking wait."

"Nightmare. I hate waiting on death. I mean, I know it will happen. It's just waiting for it to happen."

"Here you go, lads. Enjoy."

"Thanks, Heather. You're a star, hen."

"No problem. You want another beer, boys?"

"Aye and we want you to take the day off and come out for a drink."

"I'm no' sure about that."

"Come on, hen. I'm sure your old man can run this place for one day."

"He's right, Heather. You only live once."

"Ok, I will meet you in the pub about half six."

"Brilliant, hen."

Jagger headed over to the pay phone to phone Syd in the pub.

"Hello, Argosy bar."

"Is Syd there?"

"Syd who?"

"Look, he will be there. Just shout, 'Is Syd in the bar?'"

"All right, mate, chill. Is there a Syd in the bar?"

"I'm here all right. Who is it?"

"Syd, it's Jagger. How's things, mate?"

"All good here, Jagger. How you doing?"

"I'm about to kill Ringo but apart from that I'm ok."

"No' much of a roommate, is he?"

"No, but he is enjoying himself."

"Where are you?"

"Millport, mate."

"How is it?"

"It's quiet with a few good pubs. Nice wee island. Just what I need."

"That's good. Wish it was me."

"Has anyone been in looking for us?"

"No, mate, all good. The cops did come in for Ringo but it was to do with him having a lock in by himself in here."

"What do they want to talk to him about?"

"No' sure. I think he has to pay for all the whisky he drank."

"The whisky I'm sure he told us he already paid for."

"Aye, sounds about right."

"Ok, but nothing else then?"

"No, mate. It's all good. How's your eye?"

"A lot better now. How is my flat?"

"It's fine. Me and Daisy have been staying in it."

"Love nest."

"Aye, mate. We have been at it every night. My balls are red raw, mate. I'm no' kidding."

"I'm happy for you, mate. Look, we should be back home late tomorrow."

"Ok, bring me something back."

"Like what?"

"I don't know, like a holiday gift."

"I'm no' on fucking holiday, mate. I'm about two hours away from Glasgow."

"Aye, ok then. See you tomorrow."

"Bye, mate. Take it easy."

Later that day Jagger and Ringo were in the pub sitting by the fire when Heather walked in.

"Hi, boys."

"We didn't think you would show."

"Well, I told my dad I was away to see my friend."

"I'm amazed you have a friend with all the hours you work in that hotel."

"I have some."

"Aye? Any for me?"

"No, Ringo, sorry."

Jagger went to the bar to get Heather a drink. "Two pints and a gin and tonic, mate."

"How the hell did you manage to get young Heather out for a drink?"

"Easy. We told her life is too short to be working all the time."

"Her life will be short if that bastard of a dad finds out she is in here, son."

"Don't worry about him. I can deal with him."

"Aye, you can, but Heather can't. He will give her hell for being in here."

"Well, I won't tell him if you don't."

"It's a small island, son."

Jagger took the drinks over to the table.

"So, you like this table by the fire?"

"Aye. We don't get a lot of open fires in pubs in Glasgow."

"No? Why not?"

"Because if there is a fight, some cunt would get put in it head first."

"My God… I don't think I want to go out for a drink in Glasgow."

"No, you would love it."

"So, what do you do for work, Jagger?"

"I work in a kitchen."

"Washing pots."

"Ok, thanks, Ringo."

"And what about you, Ringo?"

"What about me?"

"What do you do for work?"

"I sell drugs, hen. Mostly hash or a bit of speed and that."

"Ok."

"Fuck's sake, Ringo."

"What?"

"No, it's cool. There are drugs sold here too from time to time."

"Can you get me some?"

"No, sorry, Ringo."

"You ever going to leave here, Heather?"

"Some day, Jagger. When my knight shows up."

"I hope he shows up soon for you."

"Maybe he already has, Jagger."

"Right, Ringo, your round."

"Let me get them," said Heather.

"No, it's cool. Ringo knows where the bar is."

"All right, same again."

"So, your dad won't be happy if he finds out you were in here with us two."

"*If* he finds out? More like *when* he finds out in this place. They will all being talking down the post office shop tomorrow."

"Aye, it's the same where we come from. A pub full of guys all talking shit about each other."

"Right, guys, here we go. Two beers and a gin and tonic. Fucking four pounds, ninety pence for that round. The cunt should have a mask on, robbing fucker."

"Hotel prices, mate."

"This is my last one anyway. I'm up early tomorrow."

"Aye, same with us. I don't want to be on the ferry and the train with a hangover."

"We need to get some cans for the room."

"We will, mate."

"Aye, and a chippy too."

"Cool, Ringo."

"Let me get yous boys a wee whisky for the road."

"No, Heather."

"Yes. Just to say thanks for getting me out for a change."

As Heather went to the bar, Ringo whispered to Jagger, "She has her eye on you, mate."

"No, she hasn't."

"She fucking has. I'm telling you."

"She is just being a friend, Ringo."

"She can't stop looking at you, mate. I bet she is moist right now like out of date bread."

"Fuck's sake, Ringo. She is no' like that."

"No' like what? She is female and she has needs just like the rest of them."

"You're talking like she is a cow."

"No. I'm just saying she is giving you the look, mate."

"Well, nothing is going to happen."

"Shame. The poor lass has needs."

"Well, it's the last thing I need right now."

"I bet she is leaking like a fucking broken fridge as well."

"You need help."

"Here you go, boys. Cheers."

"Cheers and thanks, Heather."

"Aye. Cheers, hen. All the best."

The boys walked Heather back to the hotel. Ringo went to the shop to get the beer for the room while Jagger waited for him at the front door of the hotel.

"Thanks for tonight, Jagger. I enjoyed it."

"Any time, Heather, and I'm sorry about Ringo. He can be a bit much sometimes."

"No, he was fine. I think he's funny."

"He is that."

"Do you think he would be ok by himself tonight?"

"I'm no' sure. Why?"

"Well, you could sleep in my room if you want."

"I can't. I'm sorry."

"No, I'm sorry. You must have a girlfriend."

"Aye. Well, I'm no' sure."

"What do you mean?"

"We spilt up and I don't know if she is coming back or not."

"I'm sorry to hear that."

"It's just I need to sort it out. I don't know what I'm doing one day to the next."

"Sounds like you want her back."

"Who knows. All I know is right now if I sleep in your room tonight then I know she is never coming back. If you know what I mean."

"I do. You're a good guy. I hope you work it out. Goodnight, Jagger."

"Goodnight, Heather."

"And if she doesn't come back, you can always come here for a holiday."

"It's a deal, Heather. And I won't bring Ringo next time."

The next morning Ringo was up before Jagger and down at the bar having a coffee and a smoke talking to Heather while she worked.

"You got a hangover, Ringo?"

"No, Heather, I'm good, thank fuck."

"What about Jagger?"

"No' sure. He was still asleep when I came down."

"You want another coffee? Maybe with a wee whisky in it?"

"You know me so well, Heather."

"Watch. Too much coffee and you will be running to the toilet."

"That's the plan."

"What?"

"Nothing, hen. Just talking to myself."

"Here is your coffee. I'm away to clean the toilets before Father needs to go."

"Aye, ok. Have fun, hen."

Ringo sat there waiting for Heather to finish cleaning the toilets and what he hadn't told her was he was bursting for a shit but he had plans for it. As soon as Heather walked out the toilets Ringo ran in. He got into the cubicle, grabbed a load of toilet paper and shit into his hand. He then rolled away all the paper till he got the cardboard bit of the end. He pulled a teaspoon out of his pocket and started to scoop his shit into the cardboard like it was fucking cannelloni trying his best not to smell it. But it was bad after a night of beer and a single black pudding from the chip shop. He took his last wee bit of shit and ran it onto the pan. He then went into the other cubicle with his cardboard shit bomb and gently put it between the pan and the toilet seat. He then headed back out to the bar and waited for the manager to show up for his daily shit.

Just then Jagger walked into the bar. "All right, Ringo."

"All right, mate. You up then, sleepyhead?"

"Why you down here? We're going to go. I got our bags at the front door."

"Just a minute till I finish my coffee."

"Since when did you get up for coffee?"

Just as they were talking, the manager walked by to go to the toilet. "Is that yous boys away then? Shame. Bye."

"Aye. Bye, Basil."

As he walked into the toilet Jagger was watching Ringo watching Basil. "Ringo, what the fuck you up to, mate?"

"Just a second, Jagger."

"We need to go and get the ferry."

"Just a second, mate. I need to know."

"Know what?"

The next thing they heard was Basil shouting from the toilet. "What the fuck? Fucking dirty smelly bastards! Ya dirty. It's everywhere. Fucking hell!"

"Right, Jagger. We can go now. Bye, Heather."

Jagger stood there in shock trying to work out what was happening then he said, "Bye, Heather. And sorry for whatever is going on."

Ringo and Jagger ran out the hotel and onto the bus to get the ferry. Once they got on the ferry to safety, Jagger asked Ringo, "Right, cunt, what did you do to Basil?"

"I set a jobby trap."

"Wait, what the fuck is a jobby trap?"

"I got the end of a toilet roll, filled it with my own shit and stuck it between the pan and the seat, so when Basil sat down in the pan for his daily shit, all my shit would pour out into his fucking pants."

"So, you're telling me that guy is sitting in his toilet just now trying to work out how to get your shit out of his fucking Y-fronts?"

"Aye. Brilliant."

"He will phone the fucking cops, mate."

"No, he won't."

"He fucking will and do you know why he will phone them?"

"No, why?"

"Because putting your shit all over some cunt is against the law."

"He was asking for it, Jagger. Come on."

"I know he was but I already told you, Ringo. We are no' the fucking A Team."

"Well, he has a big Mr T in his pants now, mate."

"I was thinking if things don't work out with Sally, I could go back to see Heather, take her out for a drink, but that's fucked now."

"How is it? She will get it."

"I can't just show up and say, 'Hi, it's me. Remember, my pal covered your old man in shit.'"

"Never mind worrying about Sally or Heather. Just take some time away from the birds and make time for your pals."

"Aye, whatever."

"I will never leave you, mate."

"Aye, smashing."

CHAPTER 8

GROWING UP OR GIVING UP...

That day back in Glasgow Syd sat in the pub waiting for his pals to come home. At the table was just Syd and two old guys watching the horse racing. As Syd sat there enjoying his pint, Del the Smell walked in.

"All right. Syd. How's things, mate?"

"I'm good, Del."

"You want a beer?"

"No, mate."

"Is it ok if I sit here?"

"If you want, Del, but Jagger and Ringo will be in soon, so don't get comfortable, mate."

"Don't worry, I won't. I don't want to be here when Jagger shows up. He has it in for me."

"Don't worry about Jagger. He is no' a bad guy."

"I know, Syd. I just feel like all this shit with Sally… he is taking it out on me."

"No, Del. He is all good now."

"My Annmarie thinks he is giving me a hard time because he has a wee fancy for her."

Syd almost spit his beer everywhere. "No, Del, I don't think your bird is what Jagger wants, mate. Don't worry, she is safe around him."

"I know a guy who is looking to sell a load of coke and I was thinking maybe you and the boys would like to buy it."

"No, we like to stick to selling a bit of hash, mate."

"There is money to be made here, Syd."

"The Crows sells coke. Go and ask him."

"I can't. I owe the Crow money. A lot, mate."

"Well, I hope you have it for him."

"Why?"

"Because him and his three stormtroopers have just walked in."

"Fuck. I'm away out the fire exit."

"Ok, mate. Bye."

The Crow walked over to the table and dugs up the two old guys. "Right, you old fuckers, away and sit elsewhere. Me and the man here need to talk."

The two old guys got up and walked away.

"All right, Syd. What's happening, mate?"

"No' much. Just in for a beer."

"Was that fucking Del the Smell you were talking to?"

"Aye, but as soon as he seen you, he got off, so thanks for that."

"Cunt better pay up soon or he will be a sorry boy."

"He has been coming to you for drugs for years. Now what's the problem?"

"The problem now is when he didn't pay up I would just fuck his bird or get her to suck my dick."

"So why don't you do that now?"

"Have you seen how fat the cow is now? Fuck that. I don't do fat birds."

"Del letting cunts fuck Annmarie is the only thing that got him through his adult life."

"Aye, well, he better send the fat cunt to Weight Watchers."

"Aye, she is no stranger to a sausage supper."

"That's fucking true. Anyway, where is your two wee girlfriends?"

"They are on their way."

"No' seen them much the last few days and the cops have been hanging about."

"Fuck all to do with us."

"Aye, so why they hiding out the way? Anything to do with the chip shop maybe?"

"Fuck all to do with us."

"Look. Do whatever you want about here, but when you have the cops sniffing about… that's bad for my business."

"We know and the cops are no' looking for us."

"You sure? They were in here yesterday talking about Ringo."

"That was because he fell asleep in here and drank a bottle of their whisky. He has to pay it back then they will be gone."

"Well, he better pay up and soon."

"I will tell him today."

"Tell your pals to keep their heads down. Some of my boys have seen undercover cops in here for a drink."

"Cops drink too."

"No, they are looking for some cunt."

"I will keep my eyes open. Don't worry."

"You know, Syd, and this is no' the drink talking, but you're a good guy."

"Thanks."

"You could come and work for me."

"No, thanks. I'm good where I am."

"What, with them two cunts? I mean, Jagger is all right, just full of himself and Ringo… well, that cunt is as much use as a dick flavoured lollipop."

"We get by just fine."

"You sure, Syd? We could be good pals."

"How could you ever see me as a real pal knowing I had turned my back on my other pals?"

"Well said, Syd, well said."

The Crow walked back over to the bar and shouted for another drink.

Syd felt like he could breathe again. "Fuck's sake, boys. Hurry up."

Just then the door opened and the daylight sun shone in and in walked Syd's two pals. Ringo headed to the bar and Jagger headed over to Syd.

"Well, looks like the love birds are back. How was your honeymoon?"

"Don't ask, mate."

"That bad?"

"Just happy to be home. Have you seen Sally kicking about?"

"No, mate, but she has been on the phone to Daisy."

"How's that going? Hope you changed my bed sheets."

"We are doing good, but her mum and dad are still having none of it."

"Fuck them."

"I know, but she is very close with them."

Ringo brought the beers over. "All right, Syd. You miss me, mate?"

"Fucking right I did, mate. The place is no' the same without you."

"Well, let's get on it tonight, lads."

"Aye. Before you get on it, you better get your money out and pay for that whisky you drank. The cops were in here talking to the barmaid about it the other day."

"Go and pay for that now, Ringo. We have enough cunts looking for us. We don't need this."

"Aye, all right, chill. I'm going."

"Del the Smell was in."

"What was he wanting?"

"Says he knows a guy who can give us a good price for a bit of coke."

"How much coke?"

"No' sure but I could find out."

"No, fuck that cunt. I want nothing to do with him."

"Aye, but we could make a bit of money."

"No, I hate that fat smelly cunt. I wouldn't give him a nod in the desert or the steam of my shit if he was cold."

"Ok, cool. Anyway, how was Millport?"

"Nice lovely island, nice wee B&B, the pub had an open fire in it…"

"Sounds good."

"And Ringo covered the manager in shit."

"What for?"

"He was a bully."

"Aye, Ringo hates them."

"So, we got out of there fast before the cops on the island showed up."

"Would probably only be like one cop, so don't worry about it."

Ringo came back from the bar with a big smile on his face.

"What have you done now?"

"Me? Fuck all."

"Why the smile then?"

"There were two girls at the bar and I got a date tonight with one of them."

"Fuck's sake, you're just back."

"Did you see how fit she was?"

"No, we didn't because we thought you were busy paying for that bottle of whisky you drank."

"I did pay for it and the two birds asked me what I had done, so we got talking and they are heading into town and I have to meet one of them later."

"Good for you. Enjoy your night."

"You know, maybe yous two could help me."

"Hell no."

"What? I didn't even say what is was."

"Ok, go on, tell us."

"Well, later when I meet this wee bird in the pub in the toon…"

"Aye, go on."

"Yous two could come in acting all drunk and loud."

"Why?"

"So I can act like the big hard man and tell yous to fuck up and get the fuck out the pub."

"No, I'm no' doing it."

"Come on, mate. When that wee bird sees me telling yous off she will want me big time."

"She has seen us in here just now before she left."

"No, she didn't. She had her back to you. Come on, Jagger. Help a pal out. If this works her knickers will be more ringing than my mum's phone when my auntie Jean from Canada has gossip."

"Get old Tash and Bob at the bar. They will do it if you get them a few beers."

"It won't look as good digging up two old guys. It needs to be you and Syd."

"I was just wanting a few beers then home to my kip. No heading into the toon."

"We could go in and get some food then head back here for a few."

"Yes, that's it. Syd is right. Make a night of it."

"Well, when do we need to do this?"

"No' yet, mate. In a few hours. Let her get a few drinks down her first."

"Well, you're buying the beer, Ringo."

"Cool, mate. Whatever you want as long as it works. I really need a bit of strange."

"That's what a married guys says, no' single guys."

"Well, ok, what do you want me to say? I hope she is as hungry as a nun's cunt?"

"You do need help, Ringo."

"No, Syd. My mum had me checked out. I'm good."

"You hear that? Some cunt in here today is a big Bob Dylan fan. They have been playing him all day."

"Can't beat a bit of Bob."

"I know, Ringo, but I' needing a joint listening to it."

"He can't sing but he can write a song that guy."

"Very true, Ringo. He is better than the Beatles."

"Too far, Syd."

"They say his song *Mr Tambourine Man* is about a drug dealer."

"It's a good song but why a drug dealer?"

"No' sure. Just the way some of the lyrics go."

"Aye, play a song for me could mean give me a hit."

"And take me on a trip upon your magic swirling ship. In the jingle jangle morning I'll come following you."

"Aye, that could be the come down and you want more."

"Who knows, but now I hope that guy at the jukebox plays it next."

"It's a bit like *Lucy in the Sky with Diamonds*. That spells LSD."

"I knew you would have to think of a Beatles song, Ringo."

"I know one about the Beatles."

"What one, Jagger?"

"I know what *Get Back* is about?"

"Ok, come, don't be shy. Tell the group."

"*Get Back* was Paul's way of saying to John, 'Get back with your pals. Get back in the band. Get this cunt Yoko to fuck off.' That's why he sings Jojo instead of John."

"Aye, he sings about a guy who is lost and sings about a bird who has it coming."

"Well, when you need to do something to get your pal back and you are in a band what better to do than write him a hidden message?"

"Aye, shame it didn't work."

"Ok, any more? I'm liking this."

"What about you, Syd?"

"I have one but it's bad."

"Sounds like this is going to be good."

"No, Ringo, it's really bad, mate."

"Go for it, Syd."

"Well, I was at a family wedding a few years back and I was sitting with all the men of the family having a good drink."

"As you do, aye."

"Well, *Brown-Eyed Girl* come on the disco and all the women went nuts and all got up to dance and one of my cousins said to me if only they knew what that song was about they wouldn't be up there dancing to it."

"What did he say?"

"Well, I said, 'What do you mean?' and he said, '*Brown-Eyed Girl* is about fucking your bird up the back door because it's her bad week.'"

"Fuck off, Syd. Sounds like your old cousin was wanting into your back door, mate."

"No, but he has a point if you listen to the lyrics."

"So, brown-eyed is her asshole?"

"Yes, Ringo. We worked that out."

"Aye, and days when the rains came is her bad week and down in the hollow playing a new game…"

"That is fucked up, Syd."

"I know, mate, and once someone tells you it you can't help but think it."

"Do you think the bit of the song when he sings 'sha-la-la la-la-la' is him trying to stick it in?"

"Who knows, Ringo."

"I'm going to play it on the jukebox."

"Did you no' hear what Syd just said?"

"Aye, I did but it's a good song and it's stuck in my head now."

"Better than being stuck in your arse, mate."

"Fuck that. Only thing that gets stuck in my arse is bags of drugs."

Old Archie the drunk guy who always sat beside the boys sleeping said, without opening his eyes, "Yous young cunts know fuck all. *Brown-Eyed Girl* is a song about a white guy who falls in love with a black girl."

Jagger, Syd and Ringo all looked at each other in shock and burst out laughing.

"Fucking hell, Archie. You awake?"

"Aye, morning, Archie. Time for work."

Old Archie took a sip of his pint and went back to sleep. Jagger went to the bar to get the beers in. He was still laughing when Syd shouted on him. He looked round at Syd and said, "What?"

Syd looked at the pub door. Jagger turned to see what he was looking at. As Jagger turned around, still laughing, he saw Sally standing by the pub door looking cold and beautiful. He suddenly felt as cold as she looked and he didn't know what to do. Sally gave him a smile and walked back out the pub. Jagger ran after her.

"Wait, Sally, where you going?"

"I'm going home, Jagger."

"Where? Your mum's home or our home?"

"My mum's."

"Why you here then?"

"I thought I should come and see you."

"I'm glad you did."

"Where the fuck have you been, Jagger?"

"I had to keep my head down for a few days, that's all."

"People are talking, saying you and Ringo are up to no good."

"That's bullshit."

"I know what Ringo is like and if you are drunk you will be daft enough and get involved in his shit."

"Well, what about you?"

"What about me?"

"Word round the camp fire is you have been out on the town with some guy."

"You got people watching me now, Jagger?"

"No. Look, why don't you come in and have a drink?"

"No, I can't. I don't want to sit with you and your pals drinking and smoking. Yous need to grow up."

"People don't grow up, Sally, they give up."

"That's you, Jagger. All rock and roll. Well I can't do that no more."

"So, we are over just like that?"

"Looks like it and I really need to go."

Jagger stood there in the cold watching Sally walk away. He felt angry at himself for not having the words to say to make her stay He wanted to tell her how much she meant to him, that wild horses couldn't drag him away from her, but he was silent. He just walked back into the pub and sat down at the table.

Syd said, "You ok, mate?"

"Wonderful, Syd. Just wonderful, mate."

The table was quite for a few seconds then Ringo said, "Of all the bars in all the world she had to walk into mine."

A few hours later Ringo was with his new friend in town. He was drinking and dancing with her. The girl was loving it and he was showing her the time of her life. As Ringo was telling her and her pals a joke, Jagger and Syd walked in. They headed right to the bar and got two beers and two Jack and Cokes.

Syd put a line out on the bar and the young barmaid said, "You can't do that in here."

Syd said, "Aye? And who is going to stop me?"

Everyone in the pub stopped to look over at Jagger and Syd.

Jagger downed his Jack then said, "What the fuck is up with everyone in here?"

Ringo's new friend said, "Let's go to another pub. They look like trouble."

"No, hen, it's cool. Don't worry about them two. They won't do fuck all."

Just then Syd shouted at the barmaid, "Another two Jack and Cokes and hurry up, hen. Fucking drink is flowing like fucking mud in here."

Ringo said, "That's it. I'm putting them out of here."

His new friend told him, "No, don't say anything."

But Ringo walked over. "All right, lads. I think it's time to go."

"Well, see you later then."

"No, pal. *You* need to go."

"And what if we don't?"

"Look and look hard. Do any of you cunts know who the fuck I am?"

Jagger looked round and said, "Aye, mate, I know. We will just have our beer then we will go."

"No, cunt. You go now."

Syd whispered to Jagger and Jagger told him, "No. We need to go. I fucking know who he is. Now let's go."

Ringo shouted, "Wait a minute. Before you go, I want yous two cunts to buy me and my friends a round of drinks."

Syd and Jagger stopped and looked round at Ringo. Jagger had a look on his face and Ringo knew he had gone too far.

"Look, pal, we are leaving now."

"No, a round first then you can go."

Jagger walked up to the bar. "A round of drinks for them please."

"Make it doubles, mate."

Jagger looked at Ringo again, the whole time his face was red but he held back. "Aye, ok, doubles."

The barmaid got the drinks and Jagger paid for them.

As Jagger and Syd were walking out, Ringo said, "Now I don't want to see yous two cunts again any time soon."

Jagger looked round and said, "No, you won't. We were here to meet our other pal but he is no' here."

"Well, away and find him."

"Don't worry, mate. I will be seeing him real soon."

Jagger and Syd walked out the pub door and Ringo's new friend put her arms around him and said, "That was amazing, Ringo."

"Aye. No cunt fucks with me, hen."

"You're my hero, Ringo. How can I thank you?"

"I'm sure we can think of something, sweetheart."

The next day Jagger was in his flat when he heard someone at the door. It was young Leeann.

"All right, pal. What's happening?"

"You busy just now, Jagger?"

"No, pal. Just going to have a coffee then head to the pub and see Ringo. He doesn't know it yet but he is buying me beers today."

"Cool. Could you come and talk to my mum? She is acting a bit strange just now."

"Sure. What's up with her?"

"She is saying the electricity company is robbing her. She is going off her head. I don't know what to do."

"It's ok. I will talk to her. Let's go."

Jagger and Leeann walked into her flat and they found Leeann's mum standing in the kitchen smoking.

"Hi, Jean. You ok, hen?"

"Jagger, son, I'm no' happy."

"About what?"

"The electricity company are stealing from me, son. I'm no' daft."

It's all right, Jean. We will work it out. Now tell me about it."

"Look at my letter from them. It's says I have to pay them three hundred and fifty-five pounds. My bill is never that high. God, we only put one light on at a time, Jagger."

"What has your bill been in the past, Jean?"

"It's always about forty-five pounds. Never any more than that, son."

"I will phone them and talk to them. Don't worry."

"It's ok, Jagger. I phoned the police. They're on their way."

"You phoned the cops?"

"Aye, son. They are no' robbing me."

"Well, ok. I'm going to wait in my flat. Let me know how you got on."

"Can you no' stay, Jagger?"

"No, but I will come back when the police are away. Don't worry, Jean."

Just as Jagger got to the door and opened it, there was a cop standing at the other side.

"Good timing, mate."

"Aye. How you doing, officer?"

"I'm good. We got a strange call saying someone was getting robbed."

"Aye, it's Jean's flat. She is here, mate."

"Officer, thanks for coming. Come in."

"Is it ok if I call you Jean?"

"Sure, that's fine, officer."

"Ok, so what's been hanging, Jean?"

As Jean tells the police officer what has been going on, him and Jagger were standing in the hall of the flat. As Jean was talking Jagger was just looking around when he saw something from the side of his eye moving. Jean and the police officer were still talking. When Jagger took a closer look he saw the carpet in the bedroom start to move, then a hand came out from under the carpet. Jagger stood there looking at the hand in shock as it headed up to pull a plug out of the wall.

Jagger tapped the police officer on the arm with the back of his hand. The cop looked at Jagger then looked to see what Jagger was looking at. As they both stood there in shock the hand was still searching for the plug. The cop pulled out his handcuffs and cuffed the hand then cuffed it to the leg of the bed. Him and Jagger then ran down to the flat below old Jean's and banged on the door.

"Open the door. It's the police."

A young tanned blonde women opened the door. "Hi, officer. Is everything ok?"

The cop just walked in right past her.

"Hey, you can't come in here."

Then Jagger headed in too.

They found a guy swinging from the ceiling. "Officer, I can explain everything."

"Aye, you can explain it down in a cell, mate."

Later that day Jagger was in the pub telling Syd what happened.

"So, he was stealing her electricity?"

"Aye, mate. He had has his hand up from the fucking floor trying to find the plug."

"How the fuck did he cut a hole in her floor and she didn't know?"

"He is a local handyman. He had been in papering and painting for her. He must've cut it then."

"The dirty fucker's stealing off an old woman."

"I know, the dirty cunt. They had it all wired up too."

"What, like his telly and that?"

"Telly, washing machine, tumble dryer and his wife's fucking sunbed."

"No wonder the bill was so high."

"Aye and see Leeann was thinking her poor wee mum was going mad."

"You want another beer?"

"Aye, cheers, Syd. And that will be the last one we pay for today once that cunt Ringo shows up."

"Go easy on him. He is in love."

"He will be in ICU after last night, getting me to buy a bunch of strangers a round."

Just then Ringo walked in. "Syd, I will have one. Cheers, mate. All right, Jagger, how's things?"

"How's things? I will tell you."

"Here we go. Look, I will pay you for them drinks. Don't worry."

"You made us look like cunts."

"Aye, but it made me look cool as fuck."

"Have you got a mark on your eye?"

"Aye. Cunt hit me last night but I got out the way."

"Who fucking hit you?"

"I don't know. Just some guys in the town who were steaming."

"So how was the rest of your night with your new bird?"

"Well, shit really."

"How?"

"Well, after yous left she was all over me. I'm no' kidding. She was like a dog with a burst ball."

"So what went wrong?"

"Well, the next pub we went to a bunch of guys started to kick off and the bar staff told them to go."

"But they didn't go, did they?"

"No, they didn't."

"And your wee bird told you to step in and sort it what with you being the big hard man."

"Aye, she did."

"Fucking hell, Ringo."

"It was bad, lads. There was like five of them. All big lads and drunk. I tried talking to them but they grabbed me and one hit me."

"So what did you do?"

"Only one thing I could do. I ran away and got the last train home."

"You're a real hero, mate."

"I wasn't getting my cunt kicked in. Fuck that. I was off."

"And now you're off to the bar to pay us back for last night."

Just as Ringo came back from the bar, a guy they had never seen before walked over. "All right, lads. Any hash?"

The boys all looked at each other then looked back at the guy who was about the same age as them.

They all said at the same time, "No."

"Come on, guys. I'm cool. I just need a bit of smoke."

"You're cool? Who the fuck talks like that?"

" Like what, man?"

"Like that. Calling me, man. Piss off, mate."

The guy walked away and Jagger noticed two guys at the bar with suits on. "Who the fuck are they?"

"Who?"

"Them cunts over there."

"No' sure. Never seen them before."

"I don't like this. Cunts we don't know asking for hash."

"The cunts with the suits look like cops."

"No, they don't. You have been smoking to much hash when you should be selling it."

"I'm with Syd on this, Ringo. They are cops, mate."

"So what? We are no' doing anything. You can't get the jail for drinking a pint, can you?"

"No, but maybe they are watching us."

"Aye, Syd's right. They could be watching us so don't sell any hash for the next few weeks."

"The next few weeks? We need the money. You already had us running away last week like fucking Thelma and Louise. We lost money because of that, Jagger."

"Well, get a fucking job then, Ringo."

"No' in this lifetime. Fuck that."

The pub phone rang and someone asked for Syd. As he went to the phone, Jagger asked Ringo, "Who the fuck is phoning him here? This can't be good."

"Maybe it's *Miami Vice* and Syd is their informant."

"Fuck up, Ringo."

"He is going to rat out his two best pals and go into witness protection, live out the rest of his days far away. Somewhere like Paisley."

"You're doing my nut in, Ringo."

Just then Syd came back to the table.

"Everything ok, mate?"

"It was Daisy. She wants to talk."

"What about?"

"I'm no' sure but it doesn't sound good."

"Maybe she has changed her mind about the witness protection programme. It's no' as good as they say, you know."

"What the fuck is he on about?"

"Never mind him."

"Look, lads, the cops are no' watching us and your bird phoned to talk. Well, go and talk. Yous are always the glass is half empty lads. Fucking hell, cheer up."

Just as Syd went to meet Daisy, he opened the pub door and held it open for two of the Crow's men. They had a hold of Del the Smell. The Crow looked at his guys holding Del then looked at the two guys in suits. He put a smile on and put his arm around Del. "Del, my old pal, long time no see, mate."

"All right, Crow. I was just on my way to see you."

"Really, Del? Good man. That's good. So, you must have something for me then?"

"Well, no' right now, mate."

"Look, you smelly cunt, if it wasn't for all the strange faces in here today I would be cutting you, ya cunt."

"I can get it soon, mate, please. I will do anything. You want a ride at my bird?"

"Hell no. I want my money but until you get me it you can run about for me and do a few odd jobs, ok?"

"Anything, mate."

"Good lad. Now away and get a bath."

"Why a bath?"

"Well, how about the fact you smell, Del, and I don't have smelly cunts working for me."

"Ok, a bath. Or can I just have a shower?"

"No, Del, a bath. And soak in that fucker till you don't smell like a dead cat at the side of the road."

As Del walked out the pub the two guys in suits talked to the Crow.

"How's things, mate?"

"All good here, officer."

"So you know we are cops then?"

"Well, you're no' trying to hide it wearing suits and drinking cokes."

"Aye, true. We are no' hiding it but we want to talk to a few locals and see if they seen anything last week down at the chip shop."

"Ask away, officer. A lot of guys in here will be happy to talk."

"What about you?"

"What about me?"

"Did you see anything?"

"No, I was at home that night with my bird."

"And what about your pal?"

"What pal?"

"The one you just had a go at?"

"Who, Del? No' sure if he was about that night."

"What about the boys over there?"

"Like I said, I know fuck all."

"Is it true you don't see eye to eye with them boys?"

"What fucking boys?"

"Jagger, Syd and Ringo."

"Only know them to say hello to in here apart from that fuck all."

"I was told one of them has it in for you."

"Bullshit."

"Really?"

"Aye, really. Now I'm just going to get back to my drink, lads."

The cops walked out and the Crow headed right over to Jagger and Ringo. "What the fuck have you been up too, ladies?"

"What you talking about?"

"What I'm talking about, Ringo, is you robbing the fucking chip shop and other places."

"No' us."

"Fuck up, Ringo. Adults are talking, son."

"Look, I don't know what the cunts told you but it's no' true."

"The cunts are CID, Jagger, and they were wanting me to stick you in."

"And did you?"

"Look, you cunt—"

"I'm getting a bit fed up here."

"Watch it, Jagger, and I'm no' a fucking grass, ok?"

"Ok, cheers for that."

"Aye, mate. Like Jagger says, thanks a lot."

"Yous boys got much hash to sell?"

"No and we don't want to sell it just now with the cops kicking about."

"Well, I know a guy in Edinburgh who has a bit for me so why don't yous go and pick it up?"

"Why can't one of your boys no' go?"

"Because, Jagger, I'm trying to be nice and give your pal a job. Make a bit of money."

"I'm up for it. I will talk to Syd. Maybe go in a few days."

"Aye, well, let me know because no cunt will be making any money selling anything just now thanks to yous cunts and never mind this few days. If you want the job then you will need to go tomorrow."

The Crow went back to the bar.

"What do you think, Jagger?"

"No' sure. I don't trust him."

"It's work and it's out the way of here for a day."

"Talk to Syd. I will be at my work."

"Talk to Syd? By the sounds of it he will be too busy with a broken heart, mate."

"Aye, well, we're all busy with a broken heart just now, Ringo."

"Will you get back with Sally, mate?"

"No' sure. Only if I change my ways."

"Like what?"

"Like everything, Ringo. No more drink, drugs or pals."

"So, she wants you to grow up?"

"Pretty much."

"Life is too short to grow up and be boring."

"Aye, I said we don't grow up, we give up."

"Aye, and take up golf."

"Aye, fuck that. The golf cunts look like their mothers' dress them."

"Getting old sucks balls, mate."

"Life is like a toilet roll, Ringo. The closer you get to the end, the faster it goes."

"True, mate. Soon we will all be members of a blowing club drinking cheap beer and stinking of piss."

"Aye, and wondering where the time went, mate."

CHAPTER 9

WE ARE ALL DOOMED...

The next day Jagger was in the local supermarket doing a bit of shopping for one. He looked into his sad wee basket that had a small loaf of bread, one tin of beans and a bar of soap. He stood there, thinking, *How the fuck am I going to fit twelve cans of beer in this wee basket?*

As Jagger looked around for stuff he didn't need, he was feeling alone and pissed off. Just when he thought his day could not get any worse he heard someone call his name.

"All right, Jagger. Doing a wee bit of shopping?"

He looked round to see who it was. It was Del the Smell.

"Fucking hell. God, no' the day," he whispered under his breath.

"You in getting something for your dinner, Jagger."

"No, Del, I'm going to get a shit load of cans."

"What, cans of beer?"

"No, beans."

"Really?"

"No, you were right the first time. Beer."

"I'm just in getting some shopping in for the Crow."

"Aye? You paying off the money you owe him then?"

"Aye. Well, I work for him now. I'm part of the gang, mate."

"No luck, Del."

"Why's that then?"

"The Crow will make you work to pay him back."

"You think so?"

"Aye. You will be getting passed about like a cucumber in a women's jail. He will work you like a slave, Del."

"It's still a job."

"Good for you. Your mum and dad must be proud."

"My dad is dead, mate."

"Is he? Lucky cunt."

"What?"

"Nothing, Del."

"Look, you want me to pick up some cans and come back to your flat for a drink and a smoke?"

"How can I say this without sounding like a cunt, Del? Hell no."

"Why no'? We could get some sounds on, have a few beers and I could get my bird to come along with one of her pals."

"Look, Del, I was feeling a wee bit fed up today and now you are making me want to kill myself."

"I'm only trying to be your pal, Jagger."

"I know, Del, but that will never happen. You're a junkie cunt and I'm no', simple as that."

"I have been off everything. Only having a smoke and a beer now."

"Look, we all know you and your bird drop more pills than a three-fingered pharmacist."

"You think you're funny, Jagger, but you should watch your mouth. I have back-up now, cunt."

"Did you just call me a cunt, you smelly wee junkie?"

"Well, I'm just saying my boys will fuck you up."

"What fucking boys? You're paying off a debt."

"I'm in the gang. Any trouble, we deal with it as a gang."

"Aye? Tell your fucking gang to deal with this."

Jagger grabbed Del by the throat, pushing him onto the fresh fruit. As he was strangling Del, a worker from the shop ran up and grabbed Jagger.

"Let him go, mate."

Jagger kept going.

"Mate, you need to let him go. He is turning blue. You're going to kill him."

Jagger let one hand go and looked to find something to hit Del with. He grabbed hold of something and looked to see what he had got. A pineapple. Jagger thought, *Fuck it*, and hit Del in the face with it and then let go of him.

Del fell to the ground. "For fuck's sake, Jagger. You will hear about this. You're a dead man."

Jagger wanted to hit him again but the shop worker stopped him.

"Look, mate, my boss has phoned the cops. You need to go now."

"Aye, cool. Cheers for the heads up, mate."

Jagger walked out the shop with everyone standing looking at him. He could hear Del shouting, "I want the manager now."

Jagger walked away, thinking, *If I need to do time in the jail, then I will do it for that smelly junkie cunt.*

That same day but in Edinburgh, Ringo and Syd were standing in a bus shelter hiding from the rain. They were across the road from the flat where they had to pick up the hash but they were early.

"So, how much hash we picking up, Ringo?"

"No' sure, Syd. Just know the address and that the Crow will pay us two hundred and fifty pounds, mate."

"It better no' be a lot."

"What's a lot?"

"Like a few bags. You should've asked him."

"It won't be a few bags, mate. Don't worry."

"I hate when you say don't worry."

"Look, why don't we go for a beer then come back and get it?"

"No, the guy said two o'clock and it is almost two, so we wait here."

"This is shit. I had a much better time away with Jagger."

"Well, sitting in a nice warm B&B drinking beer by the fire in Millport is going to be a lot better than sitting in the pissing rain in Edinburgh."

"Look, I can see a pub from here. We could go and get a beer and they might have a fire in it."

"No, we wait and get this done. Then get home, drop it off then get a beer."

"I need to pick up some Edinburgh rock for my wee brother."

"You know they sell Edinburgh rock in Glasgow."

"No, they don't."

"They fucking do. It's in the paper shop at my bit."

"Well, I bet it's no' the same."

"Do you think Irn-Bru is better here than in Glasgow?"

"No' sure. Maybe if we went to a pub we would find out."

"Ok, it's time."

"What? Time for a pint?"

"No, time to pick this up. Now move your hole, Ringo, and let's no' fuck this up."

The boys headed up the close stairs and chapped the door. A guy who looked like he had been in this flat his whole life opened the door.

"All right, mate. The Crow sent us."

"Aye, cool, lads. Come on in."

They walked into this dark empty hall. It stank of weed and booze.

"Just in here, lads."

They went into another dark room. The only light in the room was from a small TV in the corner.

"You think you could open the blinds, mate, so we can see?"

"Why? You staying for tea?"

"No, but it's just a bit dark in here, pal."

"That's how I like it. No cunt can see in and see what I'm up to."

"Who is trying to see in?"

"Who knows."

"And what you up to in the dark?"

"That's my business."

"Aye, wanking."

"Sorry?"

"Nothing, mate. So where is the stuff?"

"It's here."

He handed Ringo the bag. It was a rucksack and it looked and felt heavy. Ringo started to unzip it.

"No, you can't do that."

"Do what?"

"Look in the bag. The Crow says the bag has to stay shut."

"Why? What's in it? His soul?"

"Aye, who the fuck do you think we are? Vincent and Jules?"

"I don't know who they are, but don't open the bag."

"They are from *Pulp Fiction*."

"What's that?"

"It's a film."

"I don't watch films."

"Why you got a telly then?"

"I put the telly on because my lamp broke."

"Did you come at the lamp?"

"No, I didn't."

"Ok, time to go. Thanks for the bag. We will tell the Crow you said hello."

"But I didn't."

"Aye. Anyhow, bye."

Ringo and Syd walked out the door and headed down the stairs.

"He was a bit weird."

"What do you mean a bit? He was as crazy as a shithouse rat."

"I can still hear you."

Syd and Ringo looked up.

"We were no' talking about you. Please don't kill us."

"Aye, we were talking about someone else, mate."

The guy walked back into his flat and slammed the door shut. Syd and Ringo walked out the close and down the street to the train station.

"Syd, let's go back over to the bus stop and have a look in this bag."

"We can't. That mad cunt will see us from his window."

"No, he wouldn't. He doesn't open his blinds, the mad bastard."

"We will look in it at the train station."

"It's fucking heavy, mate. I've got a bad feeling there's more than just hash in this."

As Syd and Ringo ran into the train station to get out of the way of the rain they noticed a lot of cops walking about, all talking to the passers-by.

"What the fuck is going on here, Syd?"

"Fuck knows, Ringo, but just be cool and walk to the toilet."

As they were walking to the public toilet, a police officer said hello. "All right, lads. Where you off too?"

"The toilet, officer."

The cop laughed. "No, I mean where you off to on the train today?"

"Back to Glasgow."

"How long have you been in Edinburgh?"

"Just one day."

"One day? That's not long enough to see Edinburgh, lads."

"Aye, we just went to the zoo."

"Sorry, what's your name?"

"I'm Syd."

"Hi, Syd. And your pal?"

"His name is Ringo."

"You're no' saying much, Ringo. You ok?"

"Aye, he's just a bit backwards. I look after him."

"You his friend or family?"

"Feels like both I have known him that long."

"Your pal taking you to the zoo today, Ringo?" the cop shouted.

Ringo nodded to say yes.

"Aye, he loves the zoo, the daft cunt."

"Really?"

"Aye, he can't get enough of the penguins."

"So back to Glasgow now, is it?"

"Aye, that's us up the road."

"Ok, lads, safe journey."

Syd and Ringo walked into the public toilets.

"This is bad, Ringo. That cop knows we are up to no good."

"No, he thinks I'm daft and you care for me. You done well talking to him."

"What's in that fucking bag, mate?"

Ringo went to open it. "It's locked."

"How can it be?"

"It has a small padlock on the two zips."

"Fuck, that means there is more than just hash in there, Ringo. We are fucked, mate."

"Look, we just need to get a train to Glasgow then a taxi and we are home and dry."

"That cop is out there talking to his other cop pals about us."

"They will watch us get on the train, that's all."

"There could be anything in that fucking bag, mate."

"It will be speed or coke, Syd."

"Or a fucking gun."

"It won't be a gun, mate."

"We need to move. The cop will be waiting to see us get on the Glasgow train."

"Aye, we can't hang about in here too long. Let's move."

"Look, it is busy out there."

"Aye, busy with cops."

"No' just them. It's home time for the workers, so we will just blend in."

"Aye, keep our heads down."

"If we feel the cops on us, we split up and meet in Glasgow, mate."

"Ok, Syd, cool. Let's go."

Syd and Ringo walked out and looked at the times of the trains for Glasgow.

"There, mate. Platform 5 for Glasgow and it leaves in four minutes."

"Good, Syd. Let's go."

"Can you see anything?"

"Like what?"

"Like fucking cops."

"No, mate."

"Good. That's good. We are all good. We are ok."

"Syd, I can see cops to my right."

"Is it the cunt who was talking to me?"

"I'm no' sure. I don't want to make eye contact."

"Should we split up, Ringo?"

"I'm no' sure."

"You want me to take the bag?"

"No, mate. If they see us, it will look bad."

"I can see two cops heading this way, mate."

"We need to spilt up, Syd."

"Aye, if anything happens I will get myself lifted. You get away, Ringo."

"Why me?"

"Because you have the bag. Now move."

"See you on the train, Syd."

"Hope so, mate."

As Ringo and Syd spilt, the cop who was talking to them saw Syd walking towards him.

"Are you no' going to get the train with your pal you care for?"

As Syd went to answer him, he saw the cop looking over to find Ringo. Syd looked back. Ringo was tucked away in the busy crowd. The cop kept looking and then looked at the other cops just over to the right of Syd. Syd knew they had been set up. The cops were there for him and Ringo but the good thing was they had lost Ringo. But for how long?

The cop grabbed Syd by the arm. "You're going the wrong way for the Glasgow train, mate."

Syd looked at the cop who had a big smile on his face. Syd knew this look the cop had. It was the look of a cunt who was about to get a pat on the back from his chief inspector. Syd saw the rest of the cops were going to find Ringo. They needed the bag.

The cop asked, "Where is your pal away to?"

Syd thought for a second then thought, *Fuck it*. He stuck the cop right on his nose. The cop fell to the ground, blood pouring out his nose. Syd made a run for it. He knew he wouldn't get away but as long as they ran after him and not Ringo then he would be good with that.

As Ringo stood on the street outside the train station, he saw the cops all jumping on his pal. He stood there in the rain watching Syd get put in the back of the police van. He felt bad for Syd but there was nothing he could do right now except get back to Glasgow with the bag and get a hold of Jagger. Ringo thought for a minute. *Fuck. Jagger is going to go nuts with us.* He talked to himself as he walked away into the busy crowd.

A few hours later Jagger was sitting in the pub waiting for his pals. He was sitting beside Archie who was asleep and old Bob and Tash who had drunk in the pub forever. Bob and Tash were watching the horse racing and Jagger was looking at them wondering if him and the boys would be old pals one day, all sitting in the pub talking about the good old days thinking back to all the madness. He hoped so. He liked the idea of it. Just him, Ringo and Syd looking back at their youth.

"Where is your pals today, young Jagger?" Bob asked.

"They are on their way here, Bob."

"You look like you are missing them, son."

"Missing them? I'm fed up with them."

"Aye, I know how that feels," Bob said as he looked at Tash.

"Any winners today, boys?"

"No, fuck all, son. I would be better just giving the money to my wife than the bookies."

"It would make your life a lot easier."

"That's true, son, but I would miss all the fun sitting in here."

"Aye, it's no' easy having pals."

"Sometimes it's your pals or love."

"What? You can't have both?"

"Sometimes no'. You have to change to keep a girl happy."

"You're fucking bang on there, Bob."

"What is for you won't go by you, son. Don't worry."

Jagger wasn't worried. He was worried about how long it was taking Syd and Ringo to pick up a bag. They should have been back by now.

Jagger went to the pub phone and he phoned Daisy. "Hello, Daisy. It's Jagger."

"Hi, Jagger. What's up?"

"Have you seen Syd today?"

"No, he says he was busy with you and Ringo. Why what has happened?"

"Nothing. It's just I'm in the pub and he is no' here. It's ok. He must be running late. You know what he is like."

"Why would he tell me he was with you then you phone me looking for him?"

"No, look, don't worry. I'm sure he will be here soon."

"Did he tell you we had a talk last night?"

"No, pal, he didn't."

"Aye, well, I told him if he doesn't get it together it's over."

"I'm sure he will do whatever you want him to do. He loves you."

"Well, he better hurry up. A guy in my other job has asked me out."

"Look, Daisy, he will get it together, so don't be daft and go out on a date that won't end well. He will just get jealous and his head will be all over the place."

"And why not?"

"Is this a bad line, Daisy? Can you no' hear me? Why not? I will tell you why not. Because Syd will go fucking nuts and want to kill the cunt. That's why not."

"Aye, we will see. Bye, Jagger."

As Jagger walked back to his table, he looked up to the pub door and there was Ringo standing looking cold and done in.

"Where the fuck have you been?"

"Long story, mate."

"Where is Syd?"

"In the cells in Edinburgh."

"How the fuck did that happen?"

"I think we were set up by the Crow."

"That two-faced cunt. I knew he was up to no fucking good, Ringo."

"Aye, I think the cops were waiting on us."

"So how did you get away?"

"We split up at the train station and Syd took one for the team and hit one of the cops so they all went for him."

"And that let you slip away with the bag?"

"Aye. We had to do it. If they got hold of this bag we were both going down."

"Fucking hell."

"There is one more thing."

"What?"

"The bag is locked. We don't know what is in it."

"When is the Crow coming for it?"

"I have to drop it off just now."

"Fuck that. He is no' getting it just now."

"We don't want to go there, Jagger."

"Look, he was giving up whatever was in there, so we could all get the jail and be out his way, so fuck him."

"We could tell him to get Syd out then he could get the bag back."

"Aye, maybe, Ringo. Maybe, mate."

"Just as well I didn't get the jail today."

"Why?"

"I have a meeting at the dole office tomorrow about my sick money."

"God forbid you lost your sick money, Ringo."

"Aye, then I would need to get a job like you. Fuck that, Jagger."

"Look, away and phone the Crow. Tell the cunt to meet us in here in an hour."

"Ok. What about the bag?"

"We will take it into the lounge and put it away in the kitchen. No cunt goes in there."

Jagger and Ringo took the bag into the toilets and opened it. Jagger looked inside.

"What's in it, Jagger?"

"Everything, Ringo."

"Like what?"

Jagger pulled it all out. "Like hash, pills, coke… This bag here looks like heroin and a fucking blade."

"If the cops had got hold of the bag, me and Syd would have been put away for a few years, mate."

"This bag is a set-up, Ringo. It's full of bits of drugs and a weapon."

"Aye, he was killing two birds with one stone."

"Aye, keeping the cops happy and getting us out the way."

"But we still need to remember we can't beat him. He has back-up."

"I know, mate, don't worry. All we want is Syd out the cells. Job done. Let's go back and get a beer."

"I fucking need one after today."

As they sat and wait for the Crow, Jagger told Ringo about what Daisy said. "I phoned Daisy looking for Syd."

"Fuck, what did she say?"

"A lot of shit about he better no' be up to no good."

"What did you say?"

"I told her I was looking for him to go for a beer and not to worry."

"If she finds out about all this, it will be all over for them."

"I think it already is. She said if he doesn't change and get a job, it's over."

"What is it with birds telling us to grow up?"

"And she said there is some guy who has been asking her out and she is thinking about going on a date with him."

"That would send Syd off the edge."

"I know. He would kill the poor cunt but I told her not to do anything daft."

"Too late, Jagger."

"Why is it too late?"

"If she has said she is thinking about it that means it's already happened."

"How does it?"

"It's a woman thing, mate. They are like fucking monkeys. They don't let go of one branch till they get a good hold of the next one."

"Fair point, Ringo."

The pub door opened and in walked the Drow with six of his men. They made their way right over to the table where Jagger and Ringo were.

"All right, Ringo. You were supposed to drop something off for me."

"Don't worry, we have it."

"You have it? Well, where is it? I hope it's no' in here what with all the cops kicking about thanks to yous two cunts."

"Well, thanks to you our pal is in the cells in Edinburgh."

"I wasn't talking to you yet, Jagger, but don't worry, we will talk soon."

"Can't wait."

"Now, Ringo, you take that message and go and drop it where I told you to."

"Can't do that just now."

"And why the fuck can't you do that? You too busy out on a date with Jagger here?"

"No, I need my pal out the cells first."

"How is Syd in the cells my problem?"

"Because you set them up."

"Really, Jagger, you need to keep it down or keep it shut, son."

"Look, you did what you did. You set them up. You were never looking to get this bag back but if you want it, you need to get our pal back."

"And how the fuck can I do that?"

"I don't know or care. Go and talk to some cunt who can hurry things up and get Syd out. He shouldn't be in there."

"Aye, he shouldn't. Syd is all right. It's you who should be in the cells, Jagger."

"Why? You want me out the way so you can sniff about the young team?"

"We are done here. Look, when Syd shows up, yous cunts bring me my bag. Don't make me send cunts looking for it."

"Hurry things along with Syd and your bag will be here."

"And one more thing."

"What's that?"

"The next time you kick the shit out of Del the Smell, these cunts will be having a word with you."

"I forgot he was working for you now. Sorry about that."

The Crow walked away with his guys right behind him.

"Why did you beat up Del?"

"I met him in the shops and he was doing my nut in."

"Asking you for money?"

"No, he was trying to be my pal and my head was all over the place with Sally and all that. He wouldn't fuck off so I hit him with a pineapple."

"Wait, what did you say?"

"I hit him with a pineapple."

"Why a pineapple?"

"Because I couldn't reach the fucking coconuts."

"Just as well. You would've killed him with a coconut but you would have done us all a favour. But then you would have had a bounty on your head."

"I should have done us all a favour and hit the fucker with a bar of soap."

"It's a soap bomb that fat smelly junkie cunt needs."

The next day Ringo was sitting in the dole office waiting to see who he had a meeting with. He was hoping it was Mr Stewart. He had always been good with Ringo. Mr Stewart, like Ringo, was a die-hard Beatles fan so Ringo knew to keep him busy talking about the Beatles and not work. As Ringo sat on his seat, he was holding in a shit he had been needing all morning but he didn't want to go to the toilet just now. No, that shit he was holding was his plan B. If the meeting was going south and it looked like he was going to have to look for a job then he would just shit his pants in front of whoever was in the meeting with him and say, "Sorry I have just shat myself. I can't hold my shit in anymore," and the smell would end the meeting.

Ringo took a swig of vodka out his half bottle to make sure he stank of the drink. The office door opened and it was Mr Stewart. Ringo was so happy to see him he almost shit himself.

"All right, Ringo son. How's things?"

"I'm ok, Mr Stewart. It's good to see you."

"Come on in."

Ringo sat down to help hold his shit in.

"How you been doing, Ringo?"

"I'm still fucked with the booze, Mr Stewart."

"Sorry to hear that. Look, I have a bit of bad news, mate."

"What's that now? Don't be telling you have got me a job, Mr Stewart."

"There is someone else going to be sitting in the meeting today."

"Who?"

"She is a new member of our team and between you and me she is a wee cunt. A one for the watching. She is making her way to the top. A wee dangerous bastard."

"Smashing."

"Here she comes. Look, just tell her your problems."

"Has she got all day?"

The door opened and a young good looking girl, about twenty-four years old, walked in.

"Hi there. Sorry I'm late."

"That's ok, hen."

"Hi, I'm Jade. You must be David."

"My pals call me Ringo."

"Really? That's good."

"My mate, his nickname is Jagger because he is a Rolling Stones fan. He would like you."

"Why would he like me?"

"Your name."

"What about my name?"

"It's the same name as Mick Jagger's daughter. You know, Jade Jagger."

"Right… Anyway, David, do you know why you have been called in today?"

"No, Jade, I don't."

"Well, my job is to see if I can get you off the dole and back to work."

"I can't work."

"And why is that may I ask?"

"I'm an alcoholic."

"So, do you drink every day, David?"

"Every day, Jade. Eight days a week."

"And can't your doctor not help you with getting off the drink?"

"Well, you see, Jade, it's no' that easy. I drink to feel better then I get a hangover and I take drugs to cure my hangovers and I have been in and out the jail, you know."

"I'm sorry to hear that, David, but it's my job to help you get back into work."

Ringo thought, *This isn't going well. Maybe I should open the Bombay doors and drop my back-up plan.* "Look, hen, my head is fucking done in with life. I drink and I stink. Who wants me sitting in their office?"

"Maybe we could find you work outside?"

"What, like a building site? No, thanks, no way. My back…"

"Do you suffer with a bad back?"

"My back is as stiff as a porno cock, hen."

"Thanks for letting me know that."

"Sorry, Jade. Look, I don't know what to say here. My head is fucking going a hundred miles an hour. I think I might have a panic attack."

"Do you suffer with them too?"

Mr Stewart spoke up for Ringo. "Aye, he has bad panic attacks. The last one he had in here it was that bad he shit his pants."

Ringo sat there, thinking, *Thanks a lot. That was going to be my next trick.*

"Look, David, I don't want you to get worked up and end up in a panic but I will be looking into getting you back to work in the near future."

"Aye, cool, Jade. Can I go now?"

"Yes, but just one more thing."

Ringo thought, *Hurry up, hen. I have a turtle's head in my pants.* "Yes? What is it, Jade?"

"Do you have any job experience?"

"I'm no' sure."

"Just any jobs in the past that you were good at or like doing."

"No."

"Well, is there anything you can tell me about yourself that might help me find you the right job?"

"Like what."

"I don't know. Is there something you can tell us about yourself?"

"Well, aye, two interesting things about me."

"Really? What are they?"

"Well, one is my dick is the same length as two Argos pens."

"Really and what's the second?"

"I'm banned from every Argos in Glasgow."

"Have a nice day, David. I will be in touch."

Ringo bid her farewell and ran out the office holding his bum.

Later that day Ringo walked into the pub hoping that Syd would be there. As he walked in, he looked over to the table. It was only Jagger and Archie sleeping beside him.

"Any word, Jagger?"

"No, Ringo. Fuck all."

"He should be out of court by now."

"I know. He will show up. Don't worry."

"You want a beer?"

"I will try one. See how I go."

Ringo headed over to the bar. He asked for two beers and looked round to see Del the Smell walking over.

"All right, Ringo."

"All right, Del. How's things?"

"All good, Ringo. Did you hear me and Jagger had a fight?"

"No, I heard Jagger kicked the shit out of you."

"No, it was a fight."

"Del, a fight is when two cunts hit each other, no' when one cunt hits you and you go down."

"Aye, well, he was the one who used a weapon, no' me."

"He hit you with a pineapple, Del, for fuck's sake."

"Aye, well, it won't happen again. I have back-up now."

"Look, Del, just stay out the way of Jagger. He is no' in a good place just now. We are worried about Syd."

"Aye, he got the jail I was told."

"Aye, but he should be out now."

"He is."

"How do you know?"

"The Crow phoned some cunt in Edinburgh. Made sure he got a train and a taxi home."

"So, he should be on his way?"

"He is back. I just seen him going to his bird's house."

"Good. He will be in soon. That will cheer Jagger up."

"Aye and I seen his ex-bird out and about."

"Del, shut the fuck up. Talk like that will get you done in and it won't be a pineapple this time, mate."

"Aye, cool. Take it easy, Ringo."

Ringo headed back to the table with the beers. "Here we go. Get them while they are cold, mate."

"What the fuck was that fat junkie cunt saying?"

"He said he seen Syd going in to see Daisy."

"Thank fuck for that."

"I know but he should've came here first. He knows we are waiting for him."

"How did he get back from Edinburgh?"

"Del says the Crow paid for his train and taxi."

"We will need to give him his bag back."

"I will do that. The less you talk to him, the better."

Syd walked in.

"He is back. You ok, mate?"

"Wonderful. Ringo. Just wonderful, mate."

"How did it go?"

"I got done with hitting the cop. I need to go back though when my court date comes up."

"We will go with you. Don't worry, Syd."

"I know, lads. Thanks."

"How did Daisy take it?"

"No' good. She said we are over. She has had it with me."

"She will be fine in time, Syd."

"No. She said her mum and dad were right about me and I was to stay away from her."

"Plenty more birds kicking about, mate."

"No' like her, Ringo."

"It's ok, Syd. Let me get you a beer and a wee whisky, mate. You will be needing it after a night in the cells."

"Cheers, Jagger."

Jagger went to the bar. He looked round to see the Crow walking in.

"All right, Jagger. Syd back yet?"

"Aye, he is over at the table."

"That's good he got back ok. Now tell Ringo I want to talk to him."

"Looking for your wee bag?"

"Aye, but I don't want it in here. Too many undercover cops in here just now."

"Don't worry. Ringo will drop it off and then we won't need to deal with you again."

"You think so, Jagger? As long as your two pals sell hash, they will deal with me."

"Aye, well, that's their problem, no' mine."

"Tell Ringo to give that bag to one of my boys. I won't be there. I'm taking young Leeann out for a drink. It's her eighteenth birthday today."

Jagger stood there looking at him.

"What's up, Jagger? Lost for words, mate?"

"You need to leave her alone."

"Don't think so. I'm getting in there before every cunt does, mate."

"She is no' like that."

"Aye, well, you're no' her da, so fuck all to do with you."

The Crow walked away laughing. Jagger took the drinks back to the table.

"What did he say?"

"He said you need to drop the bag off to him."

"Aye, I will do it soon. He can wait."

"The cunt is taking young Leeann out drinking tonight."

"He is? Why tonight?"

"She is eighteen today."

"So, she is no' young Leeann anymore then?"

"No, she is just Leeann now."

"This is fucked up."

"Jagger, you can't do nothing. She is an adult now, mate."

"Ringo is right, mate. She has to make her own mistakes in love and life now."

"It won't end well for her."

"It will make her grow up fast."

"We are all doomed anyway."

"How's that, Ringo?"

"Well, nothing is working out for us just now. Our luck has run out, lads."

"Maybe he is right. What with you and Sally and me and Daisy..."

"And now wee Leeann is doing what all young girls do. She is looking for an older boyfriend."

"You see, that's how it works in life. When a young girl is looking for love, she wants an older guy but then as she gets older, she wants a younger guy."

"He might have a point."

"I'm telling you. See, when my wee brother has a pal over and his mum shows up to take him home, I walk the wee guy to his mum's car and she is all over me. Some old single mum wanting to play hide the sausage with me."

"Aye, Ringo. You're right, mate. We are all doomed."

"Last week I was sitting in here waiting for yous to show up, right?"

"Makes a change. We are always waiting on you."

"So I'm sitting here, having a beer, and at that table over there was a guy who was about sixty-five, right? And a women who was about, let's say, fifty-five and another guy who looked about forty-five."

"Ok... what's your point, caller?"

"Well, the guy at sixty-five was buying the woman drinks and talking to her, but she only had eyes for the other guy who was forty-five. So she went with him after the poor old guy paid for her drinks."

"No, you see, she might have had her eyes on the forty-five-year-old guy but he was too busy eyeing up a wee bird sitting at the other table who was about twenty-five."

"So what you're saying is no cunt wants someone their own age?"

"What I'm saying is we are all busy chasing something we can't have and that is why we are all doomed, lads."

"You're right, Ringo. An old guy was eyeing me up in the cells last night."

"But you were too busy eyeing up the young guard."

"Anyway, I will let you think about that one. I'm away to drop off this bag."

"Be careful, Ringo. Make sure no cunt sees you in that lounge."

"I will, Jagger. Don't worry."

Ringo went up to the empty lounge and took the bag out of the kitchen and walked out the lounge doors. He saw two guys watching him. He knew they were cops so he headed down the back lane and over a garden fence out the way. The last thing they needed was Ringo getting lifted with the bag after Syd taking one for the lads.

When he got to the flat, he met Del the Smell in the close.

"All right, Ringo. What you up to?"

"I have to drop this bag off for your boss, mate."

"Aye, cool. I will take it, mate. The Crow is away out with that wee bird Leeann. You know the one who stays in the same close as Jagger."

"Aye, I know her, Del. Look, just make sure he gets that bag."

"Why? What's in it?"

"Just some books I'm done with and was thinking the Crow would like them."

"Books? Really?"

"No, it's no' fucking books. It's drugs, you daft cunt. Now make sure he gets them."

"Ok, I will hand them to him myself, Ringo."

"Aye, you better no' take any. He knows what's in there, Del."

"I don't steal from my friends."

"You steal from every cunt, Del. Half your family don't talk to you because of your sticky fingers."

"Well, no' anymore. I'm getting off everything, Ringo, and going to make some money."

"Aye, well, just stay out the way of Jagger if you want to stay alive long enough to get rich."

"The only reason Jagger beat me in that fight was because of my asthma. We all have it, you know. It runs in my family."

"Del, no cunt runs in your fat family, mate. Now make sure the Crow gets that bag."

CHAPTER 10

TIMES, THEY ARE A CHANGING...

The next day Ringo walked into the pub to meet Jagger and Syd. When he got there, Jagger was sitting with old Bob and Tash, but no Syd.

"All right, Jagger. Where is Syd?"

"Don't ask, Ringo."

"Let me guess. He is away somewhere trying to win Daisy back."

"Aye. I think he is at the bus stop she goes to for her bus to work."

"So what about her second job in here? She done with that?"

"Well, I think so. If she doesn't want to bump into Syd, she would have to give it up."

"Aye, but she will still bump into Syd anyway. Even if she got a job on the fucking moon Syd would still show up."

"Aye, if she doesn't take him back, we will have to keep an eye on him."

"I will miss Daisy working in here. There goes our wee free pints here and there."

"Your pal is heartbroken and all you're worrying about is a free pint."

"Fucking right. I'm heartbroken too."

"If there is a job going, maybe you could go for it, so we still get a free pint."

"Me working behind the bar? Fuck that. I'm happy on this side, thanks."

"Think of all the tips you would get."

"Aye, I have a tip for you. If you want to sleep at night, don't fall in love with a beautiful woman."

"Wish you had given me that tip a few years ago, mate." Jagger turned to Bob and Tash, who were at the next table, "Guys, were yous married?"

"Aye," said Bob, "Twice, Jagger, and never again."

"How did you end up doing it again? One time would be plenty for me."

"Well, my first wife lied to me."

"And is that why you left her?"

"No, that's why I married her. She told me she was pregnant."

"You must've been a good looking cunt, Bob, if she was wanting you that bad, mate."

"Aye. I had a good wage. I was working in the shipyards back then and she was wanting away from her dad who was an old cunt."

"And what about the second wife? You still with her?"

"No, she fucked off years ago. Broke my heart she did."

"Did she go because you were spending too much time in here?"

Tash butt in. "No, boys. She left because he was spending too much time on her wee cousin."

"Fuck up, you. That's no' true."

"Come on, mate. I remember way back then she was a wee darling."

"Aye, ok, she was that. But look, lads, you should be learning from our mistakes."

"Aye, don't spend your whole life sitting in here. It goes by in a fucking flash, boys. I'm telling you."

"He is right. Before you know it, you will be old like us and all the birds will be gone."

"Now we sit in here putting on a bet and waiting to hear who has died. It's shit, lads."

"Talking about who has died, old Martin who drank in here... it's his funeral today, you want to go?"

"Who, us? We didn't know him."

"So? We hardly knew him, but there is a free pint and steak pie as well."

Jagger looked at Ringo. "What do you think, Ringo?"

"I think I'm never going to forget Martin. He was such a lovely guy."

"Aye, lads. We will be there."

"Just one thing yous old guys need to remember."

"What's that then, young Ringo?"

"Well, if there is free beer and maybe a wee whisky going too… well, I just hope you old cunts can keep up."

"Look, don't threaten us with a good time. We have been doing this since you were still in your old man's balls."

"Good, boys. See you there then."

"You know, they are spot on about life going too fast, Ringo."

"I know, mate. It's going by faster than a runaway train.

"Everyone will move on. We can't hold onto time."

"The times they are a-changing, Jagger."

"Aye, if only we could just stay young guys forever."

"Aye, do a deal with God."

"It's the devil you do a deal with, no' God."

"I'm sure every guy in here has wished that before."

"Every guy in here has one thing in common."

"What, they are all drunks?"

"No, they all have had a broken heart."

"Aye, nothing will hurt you more than a bird."

"Guys can be just as bad, Ringo."

"Aye, a guy can be but birds' lies hurt more than guys'."

"How's that?"

"Well, when a guys lies to a girl, he says something like, 'I'm away out for a beer,' but he has about eight."

"I have told that lie before."

"Right? But a bird can say something like, 'The baby is yours.'"

"Wow, that's a lie that will cut you deep in the heart and soul."

"Right? You see what I'm saying."

"Aye, you are saying men are cunts but so are birds."

"Aye, exactly."

"So, are we going to sit here and wait to see if Syd shows up or are we going for a free pint and steak pie?"

"Beer and steak pie, mate. We can find Syd later."

Jagger and Ringo headed down to the local graveyard. They saw the cars were just driving back out.

"Fucking hell, Ringo. We are too late."

"How are we too late? This is ideal. We just head back to the pub lounge and walk in with the rest of them."

"Aye, as long as we look sad, we will fit right in."

The boys walked back round to the Argosy and saw the cars outside the pub.

"Is this old guy... what's his name again?"

"Martin."

"Aye. Was Martin from Penilee like us?"

"No' sure. Why?"

"'Cause if he is from the pen, then we will know a few cunts in here."

"So? We just say we had a pint with him now and then."

"Aye, if he knows Bob and Tash then he should have drank in the Argosy."

The boys walked into the lounge with their sad faces on. They walked through the sea of black, looking for Bob and Tash but they couldn't see them anywhere.

"I don't see old Bob and Tash, Ringo."

"They should be here somewhere, mate."

"Aye, maybe they are still walking back from the graveyard."

"What I don't see, Jagger, is our free beer."

"You sure?"

"Aye, every cunt is paying at the bar."

"Fucking hell. If there is no free pint, then that means…"

"Aye, no steak pie."

"Look, split up and try and find Bob and Tash."

"Why we splitting up? It's the Argosy lounge, no' the fucking Taj Mahal."

"Look, we need to find them or we go."

"Ok."

Ringo walked up to the bar. "Two beers please."

"I will pay for them."

Ringo looked round and saw who was offering to pay for his beers. It was two brothers, Thomas and Paul. Two bad lads he knew from Pollok.

"All right, lads."

"All right, Ringo. Didn't know you knew our dad."

"What, your dad? Aye, I knew him from the pub."

"What pub?"

"Aye, a few pubs. He was a bit like myself. He didn't like just the one pub, you know."

The two brothers looked at each other. "Aye, that's true. The old man got about. He liked a few pubs."

"Aye, I'm sorry for your loss, lads."

"Aye, it fucking sucks, Ringo."

"I just need to give my pal Jagger his beer and I will be right back, boys."

"Is Jagger here too? Didn't think he knew our old man as well."

"No, he doesn't. He just came along with me so I wasn't alone at this sad time."

"Ok, Ringo. Thanks for coming. See you in a bit after we have said hello to everyone."

Ringo found Jagger and gave him his beer.

"Was it free?"

"Was what free?"

"The beer, Ringo?"

"No, was it fuck free and do you know why it's no' free?"

"Why?"

"'Cause we're at the wrong funeral, mate."

"You're joking."

"No and it gets better."

"What?"

"He was from Pollok and his boys are nutters."

"Who was from Pollok?"

"The guy who died. His boys are Thomas and Paul."

"Fuck, I do know them boys from way back in school but hey we are just showing our respects."

"Aye, but I said I knew their old man."

"Why would you say that? All you had to say was, 'I'm here for you on the loss of your dad.'"

"I didn't know it was their dad in the box and you fucked off and left me."

"I was looking for Bob and Tash."

"Aye, well, we should never have split up. Look what happened when me and Syd split up."

"Aye, ok. Let's just finish our drinks, smile and wave, and go."

"We can't. They know we are here. They want to have a drink with us."

"I'm no' staying here. Thomas and Paul are like the Kray twins of Pollok."

"We need to find out their old man's name."

"Aye, good idea. On you go then. I will wait here."

"No, you come with me."

"Let's go to the bar, get another beer and some cunt will say his name."

As the boys were waiting to get a beer at the bar, Thomas and Paul walked up to them.

"All right, boys. This is our mum."

"Hi there. Hope you're doing ok on this sad day."

"Thank you. My boys were just wanting me to walk round with them and say hello to everyone."

"Aye, it's such a shame, hen."

"So, how did you know my Tam?"

"Tam, aye, I knew him from the pub, dear."

"And I know your sons from way back when I stayed in Pollok."

"Aye, me and Tam had a few beers together. He was some guy."

Jagger looked at Ringo as if to say, "Don't fuck this up."

"I just feel so sad. I can't sleep or nothing. It's like a bad dream."

"Aye, but you got to keep your chin up even when you're fed up."

"Maybe you're right, son. Anyway, I'm away to help with the food."

"Is it steak pie, boys?"

"No sausage rolls and sandwiches."

Thomas asked Jagger, "Here, Jagger, how's your cousin John? No' seen him kicking about for a long time."

Jagger thought before he told them anything. He knew his cunt of a cousin John would owe them money. "Him? I take fuck all to do with him. He is the cunt in the family but every family has a cunt in it. Am I right, lads?"

Thomas and Paul both said at the same time, "We don't have a cunt in our family."

Ringo said, "As Jagger always says, if you don't think there is a cunt in your family then it's probably because you are the cunt."

Jagger looked at him like what the fuck.

Thomas walked up to him. "What do you mean by that?"

"Nothing, mate, just a wee joke. We tell it all the time."

"We don't joke today, lads."

"Aye, cool."

The boys walked away and Jagger and Ringo headed out the door and into the bar to dig up Bob and Tash.

"I can't see them, Jagger."

"That's because they are still at their funeral, Ringo."

"Aye, eating steak pie and drinking free beer."

"Grab the table, Ringo. I will get the drinks in."

As Ringo sat down, he saw the Crow walk in and he didn't look happy. He looked round the busy pub, saw Jagger at the bar then looked round and spotted Ringo and walked over.

"Fucking hell, here we go."

"Ringo, I need a word."

"What's up, mate?"

"Where is my bag you were to drop off?"

"I did drop it off, a few hours ago, to—"

"Don't say Del."

"Del."

"Fucking hell."

"What's wrong?"

"We can't find Del. The cunt is off with that fucking bag."

"You just can't get the staff these days, I'm telling you."

"You trying to be funny, Ringo?"

"No, mate."

"Good, 'cause I won't think twice to cut you like I'm going to cut that junkie cunt Del."

Jagger walked over with the beers. "What's happening?"

"I gave Del the bag this morning and now no cunt can find him."

"Shocker."

"Don't you start, Jagger. I'm no' in the mood."

"He will turn up when it's all done and you will make him work it off."

"No. Ringo will go and find him and bring him to me."

"Why do I need to find him?"

"'Cause you gave him the fucking bag."

"Aye, ok. I will find him. Cool, man."

"Don't you say a fucking word, Jagger."

Jagger just looked at the Crow as he walked away.

"This is bad, Jagger."

"How? It's no' our problem, it's his."

"Aye, but I gave Del the bag."

"No' your fault. He was working for the Crow so fuck them all."

"What is Del thinking robbing the Crow?"

"Del the Smell is a fat daft junkie who doesn't know any better."

"Aye, the buses don't go where that daft cunt comes from."

"Look, right now there is three things I want in life."

"What are they?"

"Del and the Crow out the way and Sally back in my life."

"Aye, well, if the Crow kills Del, you will get, as Meatloaf would say, two out of three but that ain't bad, mate."

"Maybe I should just get off the drugs and the drink and try and work things out before it's too late."

"She might have already moved on, Jagger. You can't always get what you want, you should know that."

"Are you just going to sit here and quote songs to me, Ringo?"

"Look, Jagger, we are all going through a hard time just now."

"I know, mate. Never mind me."

"I'm feeling it too, mate. With the cops hanging about like flies round shit I can't make any money. Fuck. I hope I don't end up suicidal 'cause I'm too skint to OD, mate."

"You could always just steal from the Crow."

"Aye, that would work."

"Fuck it, mate. We will be fine."

"Aye, Jagger. As they say, tough times don't last, but tough people do."

"Is that another fucking song?"

"I'm no' sure, mate. Might be."

"Fucking should be, Ringo."

Unknown to the boys their pal Syd was sitting outside the pub on the step drinking a bottle of Eldorado wine out of a bag feeling more sorry for himself than they were. He sat looking down at his cigarette burning out on the wet step. Just as he looked up to take a drink from his bottle of wine, he saw Daisy standing in front of him.

"I was told you were looking for me, Syd."

"Aye, hen. I was hoping we could talk."

"I don't have anything thing to you, Syd. I'm sorry it's over."

"But why, Daisy? We were good together. It was you and me against the whole world, remember?"

"It was, Syd, but not now. You and your pals will end up like everyone else in the scheme. Dead or in the jail."

"No' me. I'm going to find a job and find us a flat."

"I was told you got the jail in Edinburgh, Syd."

"Aye, but that's the last time, hen. I'm moving on from all that shit."

"Is that why you are sitting here in the cold pissing rain with a bottle of Eldorado?"

"I'm sitting here 'cause I'm missing you and I didn't notice the cold. I can't feel anything right now."

"Look, I need to go, Syd. My bus is coming."

"Where you going? I could come with you. We could get a drink maybe."

"No, Syd. Look, take care of yourself please."

Syd looked at the bus stop and saw a guy looking over. "Who is that?"

"Who is what, Syd? I need to go."

"Who is the cunt looking over at us in the bus stop?"

"He is just a friend, Syd. Don't start."

"Just a friend? Hey, pal, what's your fucking problem?"

Daisy ran into the bus with the guy but Syd stopped the bus doors from shutting.

"Right, cunt, come on out here. I need a word with you."

The driver told him to get off the bus but Syd was having none of it.

"Move, cunt. If you're a big man, let's go."

Daisy shouted at Syd, "Just leave me alone."

"Fuck you. After everything we have been through, you do this to me? I will stab your new boyfriend to death. You know I will. I'm no' giving a fuck about the jail."

"That's it. I'm getting the police, son."

Syd smashed the bottle of wine and walked on the bus. Daisy jumped in front of the guy and just as Syd went to grab him, Jagger grabbed Syd.

"It's ok, mate. Take it easy."

"Get him off my bus now."

"It's cool. He is going, all right?"

Ringo jumped on. "Every cunt chill out. Party is over and no cunt seen a thing, right?"

"Just get him away from me, Ringo."

"I will. Just you head into town with your new man and leave us to sort this mess out. You ok, mate?"

The guy with Daisy said, "I'm fine."

"Aye, well, this didn't happen."

"He was going to cut him with the bottle, Ringo."

"I know, Daisy, and it should have been you, hen. No' that poor cunt."

Jagger and Ringo sat with Syd outside the pub.

"What were you thinking, mate, going to cut some cunt on a bus?"

"Don't know. My head is fucked up with all this."

"Drinking wine in the street won't make you feel any better. You need to be with us."

"Sorry, lads."

"Never mind that sorry bullshit. Let's get you inside for a beer."

The boys walked into the pub to get a beer. As they sat at the table Ringo said, "You know, Syd, sometimes you just need to let it be."

"What, Ringo?"

"Never mind him. He has been quoting songs all day."

"But we do have a bit of good news for a change."

"What's that?"

"The Crow is going to kill Del the Smell."

"Why? What's Del done now?"

"He took that bag."

"What, our bag from Edinburgh?"

"Aye, he is off with it."

"Where do you think he went?"

"Don't know, but I bet he is sitting somewhere just now getting high with all the pals he didn't know he had."

"If they go and look for his fat bird they will find him. She is always with him."

"With a bit of luck the Crow kills her too. The fat cow."

"Hope he doesn't shoot her. It will just bounce back off the fat cunt."

"Now, now, Ringo. You shouldn't talk about an old girlfriend like that."

"Fuck you, Jagger. She is no' my ex."

"You did play hide the sausage with her, Ringo."

"Aye, but only had a BJ off her. I didn't make love to her or anything like that."

"Have you ever made love to any bird before?"

"Aye, Jagger, your mum."

"Here come the mum jokes."

"Well, it's all funny when it's about me."

"I was just fucking with you, Ringo."

"Aye, well, wait a few weeks when you're choking for a bird and maybe big fat Ammo will be looking no' bad."

"I would rather shit in my hands and clap than fuck that big bastard."

"You never know what a hungry man will eat, Jagger."

"Aye, well, I won't be eating her, that's for sure, Syd."

"Who wants another beer?"

Ringo said, "No' for me. I'm away to find a bag."

"Fuck that bag. The Crow can find it himself."

"Aye, but if I find it I can see what's left. Maybe get us something for tonight, lads."

"Just be careful, Ringo."

"I will see yous in a bit."

"Here, Syd. Have a wee pint with me."

"Yeah, Jagger. That sounds good, mate."

"You need to chill for a bit, Syd. You have just been lifted in Edinburgh. If you got lifted tonight, you would have done a bit of time for it all."

"I can't stop thinking about her, Jagger. She is in my soulmate. I see her in my sleep."

"Aye, but sitting thinking about her in a cell won't make it any better."

"I can't be without her."

"Look, the only way you're going to win her back is getting away from all this and getting a job."

"Aye. I can do that. You're right, mate. If I get a job and maybe rent a wee flat that would maybe make her see."

"Aye, in time you could get her back but you can be in here all week twenty-four-seven drinking and selling hash, mate."

"Maybe you could get me a job in with you."

"Aye, but you are trying to get away from your pals and show her it could be just you and her living a nice quiet life."

"Aye. Maybe I could head into town and tell her all this."

"Hell no, Syd. You need to stay away from her for a good bit of time or you will never get her back, mate."

"Aye, cool. I will."

"You sure?"

"Aye. Honest I will, Jagger."

"Maybe you should stay at mine for a bit so I can keep an eye on you. How does that sound?"

"Aye, sounds good, mate. Just like old times."

"Aye, Syd. Don't worry, mate. Better days ahead."

As the boys sat and had a beer, Ringo headed down to find Del the Smell and the bag. As Ringo walked into the close where Del and fat Ammo stayed he was stopped by their downstairs neighbour.

"Hi there, son. You on your way up to see Del or Annmarie?"

"I'm just going to see Del."

"You his pal then?"

"No. I'm just needing to see him about something, that's all."

"Aye? Well, he is away out."

"When did he go? Do you know?"

"About an hour or so, but he was in a hurry and looking about."

"I will just go and see if Annmarie knows where he went to."

"No' seen you here before. What's your name?"

"I'm Ringo and I'm in a bit of a hurry, hen."

"That's a shame."

"What is?"

"You being in a hurry. I was going to ask you in for a wee drink."

"I don't think your husband would like that, hen."

"He doesn't care. He is away just now."

"Really? Where is does he work at?"

"On the rigs. Always away and I'm left here all alone, Ringo."

"That is a wee shame, hen. So what rig is he on?"

"All different ones. He likes to go far away, so he gets the sun. I think he likes it in the forties. Really hot, you know."

"Aye. I don't like it that hot. I prefer a bird in her forties."

"So, you want a drink then, Ringo?"

"Aye. Just the one. Then I can go see where Del has went to."

Ringo walked into the kitchen.

"So what would you like to drink, Ringo?"

"A whisky would be nice, thanks."

"I only have vodka or Malibu."

"So why ask me what would I like?"

"I was hoping you would say vodka."

"Aye, a vodka will be fine."

As the women handed Ringo his drink her house coat fell open.

"Sorry, Ringo," she said looking at him.

Ringo dropped his drink into the sink. "Fuck this."

He grabbed her and they fell to the floor. Ringo felt he was in for a good time. The lonely housewife couldn't get enough of him. The both of them were rolling around on her dirty washing and just as Ringo had his head between the lonely housewife's legs, they heard the key going in the front door.

"Please tell me that's your sister coming to join us."

"No, that's my man back from the pub."

"What? I thought he was on the rigs."

"He is, but not just now you need to go out the window."

"Fucking hell."

Ringo jumped up onto the window and just as he was reaching for the drain pipe, the women grabbed his hand.

"I will find you, Ringo. Wait for me."

"What? Fucking hell, your man will find me if you don't let me go."

"It breaks my heart to let you go."

"I will break my legs if you don't let me go. Now piss off, hen."

She let him go and Ringo slid down the drain pipe and back into the close. He heard her man shouting as he walked up the stairs to find Del. Her man came running down the stairs and stopped.

"Who the fuck are you?"

"I'm going to see Del, mate. What's up with you?"

"You see any cunt come out here on your way in, mate?"

"Aye, some big young good looking guy left here in a right hurry, pal."

"What way did the cunt go?"

"Left, mate, and he was running."

The guy jumped down the stairs and was off. Ringo made his way to see fat Annmarie. When he got to their door, it was open so he just walked in. As he got to the front room he walked in to find fat Ammo giving some guy head.

"Fucking hell"

"Who the fuck is there? Is that you, Ringo?"

"Aye, it's me and, mate, put it away, for fuck's sake."

The guy was too stoned to notice.

"What the fuck you wanting, Ringo?"

"Well, no' that, Ammo. I'm looking for Del."

"Why you want, Del?"

"You know why, so don't fuck about."

"Well, I don't know where he is."

"And what about the bag?"

"What about it?"

"Where the fuck is it?"

"He has it, ok? Now fuck off, I'm busy."

"If the Crow finds him before I do, he is in trouble, Ammo."

"The silly cunt is already in trouble, Ringo. Fuck all you can do about it. You just want the bag. I'm no' fucking daft."

"No, you're no' daft. You're just a cow and soon to be a dead cow at that."

Ringo walked out and down the stairs, past the lonely housewife fighting with her man and headed back to find his pals.

He showed up at Jagger's flat.

"All right, Ringo."

"Apart from needing a drink, I'm fine, Jagger."

"You find Del?"

"No. Just fat Ammo giving some stoned cunt head."

"Sorry I missed that."

"Aye, that's why a need a drink. Why did yous leave the pub early?"

"'Cause, Ringo, Jagger has to look out for me and get me a job."

"What's Syd talking about?"

"Nothing. He has took a few blues to help him sleep so he is a wee bit stoned but happy."

"You all right, Syd, mate?"

"Aye, I'm good, Ringo. Jagger is getting me a job in with him, and Daisy will come back to me."

"What the fuck is he on about?"

"Never mind. Let him sleep."

"What's all this 'I'm getting a job' shit?"

"Well, I told him if he wants her back, he needs to get away from the pub and find some work."

"Away from the pub to find work? I think you forget he sells hash in the pub. That is work."

"That's no' work, Ringo. That's being a drug dealer."

"So? He still makes money."

"He needs her back. He is lost without her."

"He is fine with us, his pals."

"He will end up in the jail the way he is acting."

"So you want him to walk away from his pals and become a boring bastard?"

"No, I want my pal to be happy in a nice house with the girl he loves. What's up with that, Ringo?"

"What's up with that? What's right about it? He will get into debt buying a house and then he won't go for a pint with his pals 'cause he has to pay the fucking mortgage so he spends his weekends washing the car and cutting the grass."

"He will still meet us for a pint."

"No, he won't. His fat wife won't let him."

"Daisy is no' fat."

"Aye, but she will be. Have you seen the size of her mum's ass? They all end up looking like their mothers."

"You just don't want to lose your pal. You don't like change, Ringo."

"Maybe I don't, but I don't want my pal to give up and be miserable and then about twenty years from now she tells him to fuck off and he comes back to the pub and we are not there."

"Where are we? In the lounge?"

"No, we have moved on because we all split up. Blown and scattered like autumn leaves."

CHAPTER 11

HOLY SMOKE...

The next day Jagger was up and away to work. Ringo was up having a coffee and a smoke waiting on Syd to get up. Syd was on the sofa and Ringo was coughing to try to wake him up.

Without opening his eyes Syd said, "You want me to go to the shops and get you a packet of Tunes for that cough, mate?"

"No, I want you to get your lazy arse up and make me some breakfast."

"I don't want breakfast. I'm no' hungry."

"I never asked if you were hungry, Syd. It's me who needs food."

"Well, go and make it then and let me sleep, Ringo."

"You have been sleeping for hours now. How many Valium did you take last night?"

"Not enough, mate."

"Hey, don't be talking like that."

"It was a joke."

"Aye, good one. Now go and make your pal something to eat."

"Piss off. And anyway, there will be fuck all to eat now Sally isn't here."

"Jagger still needs to eat."

"He eats at work remember."

"Fuck. So he does."

"What's the time, Ringo?"

"It's time you got up. We have a bag to find."

"That bag will be empty by now and Del will be in the morgue."

"Well, let's get you up and out. No point sitting about here all day missing some wee bird."

"I need a beer."

"You need a wash. Now move. Jagger left a note saying get him in the pub at two."

"He say anything else?"

"Aye. Don't drink my coffee."

"How many cups you had?"

"Only four."

"He won't be happy about that."

"He will be fine with it. I will just say you had three and I had one."

"Why me?"

"Because you're all fed up and sad so I made you a coffee. Job done. Now move."

"Has he got any beer?"

"No, but the pub has."

"I could go for one now."

"I'll tell you what he does have."

"What?"

"Fucking soap. Now go and get a shower so we can go meet Jagger in the pub."

After Jagger finished his shift he headed down to the pub to meet Ringo and Syd. As he got to the pub doors he saw young Leeann.

"How you, pal?"

"I'm good, Jagger. Thanks."

"You going into the pub or leaving?"

"No, was just passing."

"How's you and your new boyfriend?"

"He is no' my boyfriend, Jagger. Anyway, how is Sally?"

"Don't know, pal. No' seen her for a while now."

"I'm sorry, Jagger. You must be missing her."

"I am, Leeann. Real bad. But don't tell anyone. I have an image to hold up."

"Always playing the big man, Jagger."

"How is your mum doing with all the carry-on with that dickhead neighbour? I have no' seen him since it all happened."

"He has been put out his flat."

"That's good and good for him. Me and the boys were looking to talk to him."

"Well, he is away and I hope he stays away."

"Don't worry, he will."

"I was at a party last night and I heard the Crow talking about what he was going to do to Del the Smell."

"I can imagine what he has planned for him, but that's Del's problem."

"He is going to hurt him bad."

"Don't take anything to do with it all, Leeann."

"I don't, so don't worry about me. I keep out of it all."

"Aye, good, pal."

"Anyway, I'm going to meet my mum. See you soon, Jagger."

"Aye, hen. I'm away to meet Ringo and Syd."

"Lucky you."

Jagger walked into the pub. Syd saw him and went to the bar to get him a pint.

"All right, Jagger. How was work?"

"Wonderful, Ringo. Just wonderful."

"Syd is away to get you a beer."

"Good. What's been happening?"

"No' much, mate. The undercover cops are still kicking about."

"You're joking."

"Wish I was, but they are still here. I don't know if they think we don't know they are cops."

"Fuck them. We are no' doing anything so let them hang about."

Syd put a beer down for Jagger. "Here you go, mate. I'm away for a piss."

"Cheers, Syd. What's up with him? He looks shattered."

"He is. How many Valium did you give him?"

"Two, I think."

"He has been sleeping more than Archie over there."

"That bad?"

"Aye. I had to give him three cups of coffee this morning just to get him up."

"My coffee? Fucking great."

"It's only a few cups of coffee for fuck's sake."

"Aye, cool. I will get more from my work."

"Think you could get me some?"

"No."

Syd came back to the table.

"You feeling any better, mate?"

"No, you don't feel anything with a broken heart except your broken heart."

"Sorry I asked."

"No, I'm fine, mate."

"Any word on Del the Smell?"

"Still on the run."

"He better stay on the run."

"Aye. Word round the campfire is the Crow is going to do him in just to let every cunt know not to fuck with him."

"Maybe you should stop having a dig at him, Jagger."

"I have fuck all to say to him, Syd."

"What was Del thinking? He must've known he would get done in for taking that bag."

"He is a useless cunt. If he fell into a barrel full of tits he would come out sucking his fucking thumb."

"He will be carrying that blade that was in the bag."

"The Crow will take it off him and stick it up his hole."

"Aye, he will do him with it 'cause Del is no' like us."

"What do you mean us?"

"Well, me then."

"Why? What's the difference from the Crow doing you to Del?"

"Well, Jagger, you see I'm no' a cunt. The Crow would have to think twice about coming for me, mate."

"Why, Ringo? What would you do if the Crow was going to do you?"

"I would do him first."

"With what? A blade?"

"No, with you know what."

"What's that mean?"

"Never you mind, Syd, and go back to sleep."

"With your old man's gun?"

"Fuck's sake. Just tell the whole pub, Jagger."

"If you were doing him with that, you would need to hit him over the head with that old piece of shit."

"Don't start. I told you it still works."

"The last cunt who got shot with that old gun was Billy the Kid."

"If I put it in your face, you would shit your pants."

"I would get you some WD-40 for it first."

Tash and Bob walked in to get a beer. Bob went to get the drinks in and Tash sat down at the table beside the boys.

"All right, lads. What's up?"

"Fuck all, Tash. How's you, mate?"

"I'm good, son. Here, Ringo, there was a guy in here last night asking about you."

"Aye? Do you know who he was?"

"No, son."

"What the fuck you done now, Ringo?"

"Fuck all. It might just be the cops who are hanging about."

"No, he was no' a cop, Ringo. One of the boys at the bar said he works on the rigs."

"You're fucking kidding…"

"No, honest, son. He was in here and he wasn't happy."

"Why was some stranger looking for you? What the fuck did you do?"

"It's no' what did I do, but more who did I do or even whose wife did I do."

"When did you find the time to fuck some cunt's wife?"

"When I went looking for Del."

"Right, keep going."

"It was Del's downstairs neighbour. She told me her man was working on the rigs and she was a bit lonely."

"Well, that was nice of you to give her some company, mate."

"Aye. Well, what she didn't explain was he did work on the rigs but not just now so just as I was getting in about her he came home."

"What did you do?"

"What I always do. I jumped out the window and down the drain pipe."

"Good for you, son."

"Thanks, Tash."

"Well, she must be missing you, son, 'cause she told her husband all about you."

"Tash, do you think this cunt will come back looking for him?"

"No, Jagger, don't worry. I put the wind up him. I told him about yous boys and made out how no cunt fucks with yous."

"And did he buy it?"

"Aye, he only had one beer and he was off out the door."

"Good man, Tash. Ringo, go and get Tash a beer."

"Aye, cool, thanks. Tash, two beers for you and Bob."

"Fuck him. He done fuck all."

Ringo got everyone a drink and as he came back to the table he told Jagger, "Father Joe is in. He is at the bar."

Father Joe was the local priest who would pop into the pub from time to time for a wee whisky and to see how everyone was doing.

"Why is Father Joe in? I was told he was off the drink."

"He is, but he has taken up having a puff."

"Ringo, don't tell me you are selling hash to a priest."

"Fucking right. Every cunt's money is the same."

"That's no' right."

"That's just because the school we went to brainwashed us. You are thinking we can't give Father Joe drugs, what would God say and all that holy bullshit."

"Aye, true. Maybe he is just smoking to save up the ash for Ash Wednesday."

"He should just help clean the ash trays in here."

"How much is he smoking?"

"No' much. About a deal a week. But he can't roll so he pays me to roll his joints for him."

"Fuck's sake, Ringo. You will be doing communion next."

"If he would pay me, I would, mate."

"Do you have his joints for him with you?"

"Aye, how?"

"Give me one and make sure he gets us a pint. He owes me, that fucker."

"Why does he owe you?"

"He told my ma years ago he seen me kissing a wee bird behind the chapel."

"Who was it? Do I know her?"

"Aye, it was your sister."

"Fuck off. I'm away to see him. All right, Father, how's tricks?"

"All good, Ringo, and how's you and the boys?"

"Aye, good. Here, stick these in your vestment, Father."

"God bless you, Ringo. You are a good lad no' matter what everyone says about on a Sunday after mass."

"You still off the whisky?"

"Yes and I feel a lot better for it."

"Aye, better just having a smoke."

"I was told there was a bit of trouble happening in here, Ringo. I hope you are not involved."

"Me? No, Father, no way. Me and the boys just do what we do and have a beer."

"Good. I have buried too many sons over the years and had to watch their poor mothers cry, so I don't need any of yous boys going the same way."

"No' us, Father. We are just here for the beer and the banter, but the cops have been hanging about, so maybe from now on I should drop them joints off at the chapel house."

"Sounds good, Ringo. Now let me get yous boys a beer before I go."

"God bless you, Father. You are a good guy."

Ringo took the beers over to the table. "Here you go, boys. Father Joe said hello."

"God bless you, Joe."

"Remember when we were wee guys and we would drink the chapel wine?"

"I loved that wine."

"Aye, it was almost as good as Eldorado."

"Still can't believe old Father Joe is puffing hash."

"Just look at it as holy smoke."

"It seems like yesterday we were little kids and were all drinking the chapel wine."

"Aye, time is flying by, lads."

"I remember it as simple times with no' a worry in our heads."

"Aye, it's sad how we forget about being a kid and enjoying ourself in the summer school holidays, playing hide and go seek or climbing a tree."

"Building a den."

"Then you get to thirteen and have a smoke and a can of beer."

"Then before you know it you're twenty-two drinking and smoking hash every fucking day and taking pills and coke at the weekend just to feel normal."

"Aye, being a wee kid seems like a hundred years ago."

"And now we have the cops watching us, all our birds have fucked off and we sells drugs to Father Joe."

"May God forgive our souls."

"Well, look who it is."

Fat Annmarie walked into the pub. She was standing alone looking around. She walked over to the table with the bag in her hand. "Hi, Ringo."

"All right, hen. I hope that is full."

"It's no'. That fucking cunt has took it all."

"So why you in here with a fucking empty bag? If the Crow walks in he will hurt you just to get to Del."

"I don't know what to do. It's no' my fault my boyfriend is a fucking nightmare."

"Look, you better go, hen, for your own good."

"Ringo, can you tell him it's fuck all to do with me?"

"I will, but get out of here and bin that bag. That will just piss him off seeing that."

"I'm a bit skint, boys. Any of yous want a BJ for a tenner?"

"No, thanks."

"You sure, Jagger? Bet you have no' had one for a while."

"The sooner the Crow finds you and your fat junkie boyfriend, the better."

"You don't even like the Crow."

"Aye, the enemy of my enemy and all that. Now fuck off."

"Yous are all a bunch of poofs."

"Ok. Bye."

As Annmarie walked out the pub, two good looking girls walked in.

"Hello, ladies…"

"Chill, Ringo. Let them sit down first, will you?"

"I'm just looking, Jagger."

"You don't stop, do you?"

"What do you mean by that, Syd"

"Well, it was only yesterday you were winching some lonely housewife's fanny on her kitchen floor and now you are eyeing up some wee bird in here like she is Sarah Connor."

"Aye, Syd is right. You can't help yourself. You think like a dog."

"So how does a dog think?"

"A dog only thinks about two things. Can I shag it or can I eat it?"

"I would eat that wee bird at the bar all night. I wouldn't get off of her till the neighbours complain about the smell."

"You could have saved yourself some time and took that BJ from fat Ammo."

"No, thanks. I'm no' looking for a quick fix. I'm looking for love."

"If the price was right, fat Ammo would love you all night."

"No, Syd. You see, fat Ammo is like the outside of a loaf of bread. Everyone has touched her but no cunt wants her."

"Well, just leave the wee birds alone for now. We are having a boys' night."

"Since when?"

"Since now. Ok, we are having beer and joints and we are just chilling."

"Why?"

"'Cause the last few days have been madness and I would like a bit of chill. What about you, Syd?"

"Sounds good, Jagger. Maybe we could get a few beers and rent out a video for tonight. Just the boys."

"Well, that sounds just wonderful, guys. I can't wait."

"Gets us away from here, Ringo."

"We are in here every fucking day, Syd, so why leave now?"

"'Cause Jagger has an empty."

"He has had an empty for a few weeks now and by the looks of it he will have an empty for a few more."

"Cheers, Ringo."

"Next you will be telling me we are getting popcorn and ice cream too."

"I might have a choc ice that's been in my fridge freezer since I moved in."

"Smashing. Look, can we just go into the piss smelly toilets and have a line please?"

"I'm up for that."

"Aye, whoever takes the smallest line, buys the next round."

"Deal. Let's go. Tash, watch our beers, mate."

"Will do, boys. Have fun."

The boys went into the pub toilet and looked for the cubicle that didn't have shit or sick all over it.

"This looks like the best one, boys."

"Aye, just give it a flush, Ringo."

"There, that's better."

Syd put out three lines of coke. The first line was not too big, the second line was bigger and the third line overtook the both of them.

"Right, who wants to go first, lads?"

"You can go first, Jagger."

"Thanks, Ringo."

Jagger looked at the three lines for a few seconds.

"Hurry up, Jagger. The pub shuts at twelve, mate."

"Right, give me a minute, for fuck's sake."

"What you thinking, Jagger?"

"Well, Syd, that is three different lines. I see here the first line is a 'Saturday morning help your hangover' line and the second line is a 'Saturday night I know no cunt at this party so I'm going to sit in the bathroom' line and the third line is a 'the love of my life has left me and I don't see her coming back any time soon so I'm going to get off my tits' line."

"So, what one you going for?"

"Well, tonight, Syd, I'm going for line number three, mate."

"No luck, Ringo. You're getting line one, mate."

"How's that, Syd?"

"'Cause I'm next, mate."

Ringo went in to take the last line. "I fucking hate coke, lads, but I love the smell of it."

As the boys were fixing themselves making sure they didn't have white power anywhere, they heard a guy going into the next cubicle.

"Shh, he might be a cop."

"So what?"

"So, we don't want him to see us all in here."

"Aye, he might think we are gay."

"No, Ringo, he might think we are taking drugs."

"Aye, that too, Jagger."

"It sounds like he has the shits."

"Aye, the beer in here will do that."

"So, if he has the shits does that mean he is a cop?"

"No, why?"

"So why tell me some cunt has the shits?"

"Look, let's just flush the pan and walk out."

"Aye, play it cool."

"Let's go."

When the boys got back to their table, Jagger told Ringo, "It's your round."

"How's it my round?"

"You lost the game."

"What game?"

"The coke line size game. Now move."

"The two wee birds that Ringo had his eye on are enjoying themselves by the looks of it."

"Aye, Syd, but they won't be when Ringo moves in on them."

"Heads up, Jagger, here comes the Crow."

"All right, girls. What's happening?"

"No' much, mate. What about you?"

"Just in for a few then off into town. Fuck sitting in here all fucking night."

"Aye, only sad cunts do that."

"Aye. Well, you said it no' me, Syd."

"You found your pal Del yet?"

"No, I haven't and he is no' my pal, Jagger, ok? So don't be a funny cunt."

"I was only asking 'cause his bird was in here no' long ago."

"Really? Here, Ringo, any of them beers for me?"

"No, sorry, mate."

"You no' think of giving me a phone and telling that fat cow was in here?"

"She is no' long away, mate."

"So what did she say?"

"Just that Del has tanned all the stuff that was in the bag."

"That fucking junkie cunt."

"She said it was fuck all to do with her."

"Aye, right. She would have been helping herself to it as well, wee fat cow. Wait till I get my hand on them."

"Like I said, you just can't get the staff these days."

"Fuck up, Jagger, or you will be a sorry boy."

"You going to look for her then?"

"Aye, but no' tonight. I'm busy. Ringo, maybe you could go and find them."

"No, you're all right."

"There will be a reward in it, mate."

"I don't know where they will be."

"They will be hanging about some junkie flat. I'm sure you know a few."

"Ringo is busy tonight too."

"Aye? Doing what?"

"Sitting in here."

"No, it's movie night tonight."

"Movie night? What the fuck you doing? Going to the cinema, having popcorn and watching *Grease* like a bunch of wee girls?"

"No, I'm thinking *Pulp Fiction* and having a choc ice."

"Aye, enjoy your choc ice, girls. I'm away into town like a real adult."

As the Crow walked away, Syd asked, "We are no' going to the cinema, are we?"

"Hell no, Syd. I hate the fucking cinema, mate. In fact the only thing I don't miss about going out with Sally is going to watch some shit film."

"Aye, it's no' even the film sometimes. It's the cunts sitting beside you stuffing their fat faces with shit like they have never eaten before."

"And even if it's a good film you want to see and wait a few weeks for it no' to be too busy, you go in, sit down and it's empty and you think, *This will do.* Then a big gang of cunts walk in and sit right beside you."

"Aye and you need to move 'cause you have a few cans of beer in your bag and if they see it, they will grass you up."

"Aye, the cinema is shit."

"So, what film are we watching later then?"

"We are no' going to the cinema, Syd. For fuck's sake."

"No, when we get back to the flat later."

"Syd is right. We will be up all night with the powder, so we could have a joint or two and watch a film."

"Aye, ok. Sounds good."

"So what film then, boys?"

"My favourite film is *The Godfather Part II*."

"Nice, Syd, but we would need to watch part one first. It's no' right putting on the second one without watching the first one, mate."

"So what about you, Ringo? Let's hear it."

"My favourite film is *The Shawshank Redemption*."

"Nice, Ringo. Good film."

"Could come in handy for you watching that, Ringo."

"Why, Syd?"

"Well, if you keep robbing shops at gun point, you will be living it."

"What's your film then, Jagger?"

"*Heat.*"

"Another good but long film."

"It's no' as long as *Shawshank.*"

"Almost. So why *Heat*?"

"I like the story of how they stick by each other but at any moment they might need to walk away from it all and never see each other again."

"I thought *Pulp Fiction* was your favourite film."

"No, he tells cunts that to sound cool."

"It is up there in my top five."

"So which one are we picking? I have them all on video."

"Good, 'cause I hate the cunt who works in the video shop. He is a wanker."

"Why? What did he do to you, Ringo?"

"Well, a few weeks back, my ma and da were out so I thought I would get some beers and a dirty film from the video shop."

"Sounds like a good night, mate."

"Aye, so I went in with my bag of beers and picked a video from the top shelf called *Big Jugs.*"

"Dirty."

"So I take it up to the counter and the guy gives me the look like, 'Aye, mate. A wee bag of beers and a blue movie,' but when I got home and put in on, turns out *Big Jugs* was a fucking documentary about Egyptian vases."

"No way."

"Aye and that cunt in the shop he fucking knew it."

"Did he say anything when you took it back?"

"No, it was some young bird that was on and she just smiled as if I wasn't the first cunt to hire the video."

"So, anyway, what film we watching tonight?"

"No' sure. See how we feel later."

"This sounds like it's going to be a smashing night, boys."

"Ok, Ringo, away and talk to them birds before it's too late."

"Now you're talking, Jagger. Right, boys, let the dog see the rabbit."

Ringo headed right over to the two girls sitting in the corner. "Hello, ladies. What's happening?"

"Nothing much, just having a drink."

"Do you believe in love at first sight or should I walk past again?"

"You will need to walk past a few times, pal."

"That's no' nice, hen."

"Never mind her. I like your shirt."

"Aye? Have a feel. You know what it's made of?"

"No. What?"

"Boyfriend material."

"I was told you were a bad boy and I shouldn't talk to you."

"Me? No. Who said that?"

"Someone who knows you."

"Only thing bad about me is my chat-up lines."

"Susan Smith. She told me."

"Wee Susan? She is nippier than a Fisherman's Friend. Don't listen to her."

"That's a shame 'cause I like a bad boy."

"Well, you're in the right place."

"Is your pals no' coming over for a drink?"

"No, they are busy talking about movies."

"I like movies too."

"You will love it in here then."

As the night went on, Jagger and Syd sat and watched Ringo do what he does best.

"He has them girls eating out of his hand."

"Aye, Syd. You should go over and join them."

"No, mate. It doesn't feel right yet."

"That's ok, mate. It takes time."

"I know it is over with Daisy, but if I was sitting over there and she walked in here and seen me, then it would be really over, if you know what I mean."

"Aye, Syd. I know, pal."

"It sucks big time, Jagger."

"It will get better in time, Syd."

"I don't know how to get over someone."

"You need to move away. Get them out of your life."

"Aye, I don't want to spend my days trying no' to bump into her. That would be a nightmare."

"Every man makes the same mistake. They hang around and watch the love of their life become a cow."

"Aye. That kind of heartbreak cuts you in half, mate."

"Need to just go. Don't hang around. Sometimes life is as hard as you make it, Syd."

"Anyway, let's get some beer and watch a film."

"What about, Ringo? We will see what he is doing. Staying or coming with us."

"I'm sure he will be staying."

"Aye. Maybe we should stay and keep an eye on him."

"I will ask him if he is staying here."

As Syd walked over to the table, he saw a girl standing at the door. He looked up at her then he turned and looked at Jagger. "Jagger, mate, look who is here."

"Who, Syd?"

"Over at the door."

Jagger stood up and looked over to see Sally standing there looking drunk and beautiful. Jagger stood there frozen. Syd gave Ringo the eye. He looked over at Sally then looked over at Jagger just standing there.

"Jagger, get back on the clock, mate."

Jagger snapped out of it and walked over to Sally. "Hey, you ok?"

"I'm ok, Jagger. You?"

"I'm no' bad. What brings you in here?"

"I need to get some of my things from the flat."

"You can go to the flat whenever you want. You don't need to ask me. It's still your flat too."

"I know, but I have been putting it off."

"And now you're drunk. You have a bit of Dutch courage?"

"Something like that, yes."

"Ok, let's go. Syd, mate?"

"Aye, Jagger?"

"You're babysitting Ringo."

"Cool, mate. See you tomorrow."

Jagger and Sally got a taxi back to their flat. When they got in, the flat was cold and dark.

"Want the fire on? It's cold in here."

"Yes and a light on too."

"I was going to keep the lights off. Didn't think you would want to see me."

"No, I need to see you."

"Cool. You want a drink or you in a hurry?"

"I will have a beer if you are having one."

"Beer sounds good to me."

"Are you going to keep this flat, Jagger?"

"Well, that depends."

"On what?"

"On you staying here with me."

"Don't do that."

"Do what?"

Jagger handed Sally her beer and she took a sip of it. Jagger took it right back off her, put the beer down and grabbed Sally. They both held onto each other for a few seconds then Sally said, "I don't think I'm coming back, Jagger."

"I know, but let's not talk about it just now. Let's just stand here holding each other."

"It felt good when I seen you sitting there in the pub."

"Me too, Sally. When I seen you it felt as good as a hot water bottle on a cold night."

"Now I need a real drink, no' a beer."

"I have whisky."

"Sounds like a bad idea."

"But fuck it."

"Ok, one won't hurt."

As the two of them sat and had a drink on the floor, the night, for the first in weeks, goes by too fast. As Sally stopped talking, Jagger took her hand, stood up and they walked into their bedroom.

"What you doing, Jagger?"

"Nothing. It's just bedtime."

"I'm no' sure we should be doing this."

"It's ok. We will worry about it tomorrow."

As he lay her down on the bed they were looking at each other's eyes.

"You ok?"

"I am."

"Good. So this is happening then?"

"Just one thing, Jagger."

"What's that?"

"I haven't shaved my legs all week," Sally said laughing.

"Don't worry about that. When I was a wee guy I would lick lollipops that fell on the carpet."

"Smashing, Jagger."

CHAPTER 12

JAIL, BAIL AND TIME TO SAIL...

The next morning Jagger woke up to find Sally had already gone. He looked around the room, trying to remember it all from last night, trying to work out if it was all just a dream. Then he saw a note at the side of the bed. It said: "Wild horses couldn't drag me away."

At the same time Syd was sitting in the pub alone waiting to see if any of his pals would show up for the hair of the dog. As he was sitting there alone, the door of the pub opened. He was hoping it was Jagger or Ringo or even better Daisy but it was the Crow and he headed right over to Syd.

"All right, Syd. What's happening?"

"Nothing much, mate. Just trying to shake off a hangover."

"Aye, I'm the same, mate. I was up the town all night. Fucking great night. You should come out with us some time. You would love it."

"Aye, sounds good."

"Better than sitting in this shithole all night. No birds in here."

"No, there was a few birds in last night. Me and Ringo were with them."

"You get your hole then?"

"No, mate. I was just out for the company."

"So you still missing that wee bird you were with?"

"Daisy. Aye, still hurting, mate. Thanks for asking."

"You would soon forget about her if you were in the toon with me, mate. Plenty of birds in the club I go to."

"Sounds brilliant, but I like it in here."

"Look, if you are wanting to get that wee bird back then you need money and lots of it. So, why don't you come and work for me?"

"I'm good, mate, but thanks."

"Look, you and Ringo are making shit money. That wee bird wants a nice wee flat and maybe a car. You could give her all that working for me."

"Let me think about it."

"Look, I'm going to get a beer, but one last thing 'cause I like you, Syd. There is a job going today. Two of my boys are going to get drugs and money off some cunts. If you want, you can go with them."

"Why would you need me? Is it no' your drugs and money I take it?"

"No, it's no' like that. I just don't trust them. They are trying to make a name for themself and I have a feeling when my boys show up they will set about them."

"So why you only sending two guys? Just send all your boys."

"I only need to send two because they will be packing, if you know what I mean."

"You want me to go and pick up money and drugs with a gun?"

"Keep it down, Syd. Aye, it will be a quick job, mate. In and out."

"No, thanks."

"There is six hundred pounds in it for you and plenty more where that came from if you are working for me."

"I'm no' sure, mate."

"Just think, if you do one or two jobs for me a week, you will have all the money you need to get a flat and take your wee bird away on holiday."

"And what if these cunts don't hand over the money and that?"

"Well, you show them you're packing and they will shit themself. Easy as that."

"I don't need to shoot anyone?"

"No, easy, cowboy. You don't. You are just there to look hard, mate. In and out."

"It would be good to get away somewhere nice with Daisy."

"Fucking right it would, Syd. Some good money is all you need."

"When is this happening?"

"Today, mate. One of my boys will phone the pub and if you are up for it, he will pick you up outside."

"No, he can pick me up round the corner."

"That's cool, Syd. He will phone the pub so don't get too drunk today."

"What if I change my mind?"

"That's ok. He will just pick up one of my boys, ok, mate? Don't worry about it. Have a beer and think about that holiday. I'm away for a beer."

Archie woke up and looked at Syd sitting there, his mind going crazy. "You ok, son?"

"Who, me? Aye, Archie, I'm fine. And good morning by the way."

"You should stay away from that boy. He is bad news, son."

"Who? The Crow?"

"Aye, him."

"He is all right. And how do you know he is bad news? You are always sleeping in here."

"My eyes might be shut but my ears are always open, son."

"He knows how to make money."

"And he knows how to get guys like you to do his dirty work."

"Look, Archie. Ringo has just walked in. He is at the bar, so don't say anything about the Crow, ok?"

"Nothing to do with me, son. Just think about what you are about to get into... that's all I'm saying."

Ringo walked over. "All right, Syd. You look like you need a beer, mate."

"So, do you how did you get on last night?"

"No' bad. Where did you go?"

"Just got off. I wasn't in the mood to stay out."

"Have you seen Jagger today?"

"No, he must still be with Sally."

"Aye, having her for his breakfast."

"If they are back together then that is some good news for a change."

"Aye, I hope so, Syd. He will be as happy as a dog with two dicks right now. Jammy fucker."

"You out for the day, Ringo?"

"Aye, mate, what else would I be up to?"

"Just asking, that's all."

"Why? You no' out all day?"

"No' sure. I have a few things to do."

"You better no' be going to look for Daisy on the bus again, Syd. I'm telling you, mate."

"No, I'm no' going looking for her, all right? So just leave it."

"Aye, ok. Chill, mate."

"There is Jagger coming in now."

"All right, boys. All right, Archie. How's life, mate?"

"Taking forever, Jagger."

"How's you today, lover boy?"

"Wonderful, Ringo."

"What? Are you feeling wonderful or you just taking the piss?"

"Who knows, Syd. My head is up my ass, lads."

"How did it go with Sally then?"

"Well, she stayed the night but when I woke up this morning she was already away."

"That sounds like a country and western song my ma plays all the time."

"Probably is, mate."

"So, you back together?"

"No, Syd. I'm right back to where I was yesterday, mate. Except today I have a hangover so bad that on the way here I had to ask the fucking lollipop man to help me get across the road."

"That bad?"

"Aye, Ringo. It's that bad I was running away from empty crisp packets blowing in the wind. Good at the time, as my old dear always says. John Wayne at night, big Wayne in the morning. Anyway, how did you get on?"

"No' much better, mate. Think I had way too much drink and coke."

"Why? Where you sick on her or something?"

"No, it was all going well till we got to bed. Then I couldn't... well, you know."

"No. What?"

"You fucking know what."

"Did you get a floppy disc, mate?"

"Aye, it was like trying to play snooker with a rope."

"Fucking hell, mate. You need to take it easy."

"She was a good looking wee bird as well, Ringo."

"I know, Syd, and she was asking me, 'What's happening? What's wrong? Is it me?'"

"Poor girl. She would have been thinking you didn't fancy her."

"I know and the more she was asking me, the more I was overthinking it all. It was a nightmare, lads."

"All this talk is making my hangover give me the fear. I need a real drink."

"I will get you a drink. What you want?"

"I will have a port and brandy."

"Why that?"

"An old guy once told me if you have a real bad hangover and want it gone, have a port and brandy. It will sort you out."

"I will have one."

"That's three then, boys. I will get them."

"Cheers, Syd."

Archie spoke up. "When I was a young guy working in the shipyards, we would get a penny drip before work to help our hangover."

"You still awake, Archie?"

"I'm telling you. And it worked."

"Here we go, lads. Three port and brandies."

"So, Archie, what the fuck is a penny drip?"

"It was all the slops in the pub. You know, all the leftover beer and whisky. It was all in a bucket and the barman would put his cloth into it and then squeeze it into your glass for a penny."

"Fuck that. We will stick with a port and brandy, Archie."

"So, Jagger, did you get a floppy disc last night or did you just sit and talk the night away?"

"No, Syd. Me and Sally had a beer and too many whiskeys then she fucked me like she owed me rent money and then she vanished like a dream."

"Sorry, mate."

"It is what it is, lads."

"Here, that bird I was with last night, her sister had an eye for you, Jagger."

"Was she good looking?"

"She was all right."

"She wasn't. I seen her."

"Thanks, Syd."

"You would shag her, Syd."

"I wouldn't even ride her into battle, Ringo."

"Well, I was going to have a threesome with her and her sister."

"But your dick didn't want to."

"No, it didn't. Shame as well. Could have been a fun night."

"That would only happened if the good looking sister was up for it."

"She would have been. I know how to talk birds into threesomes."

"Why? You had a few of them then?"

"Yes, Syd, I have."

"No, you haven't."

"I fucking have, Jagger."

"Like with who?"

"Well, a wee bird I met in town once. She took me back to her pal's for a threesome."

"What was his name?"

"It was a bird, Syd. Ok?"

"The only threesome you have ever had was when you were shagging wee Linda Smith on her sofa and her big Labrador dog walked in and started to lick your arse."

"That was some ride, boys."

"Wee Linda Smith… Now she was hotter than a Puerto Rican picnic."

"She was a good looking girl. I remember her."

"If I had no' been getting drunk and stoned all the time, things could have worked out with me and Linda."

"Who do you miss more, her or her dog?"

"Funny cunt. Well, Syd, I remember you went with her mum."

"I don't remember that."

"I do as well, Syd."

"For fuck's sake. We have all went with some cunt's mum leave it out."

"I seen her the other day out with her shopping trolley. You should get her out for a date to the bingo and make Daisy jealous."

"No, thanks. I still see her kicking about. She gives me the fear. Makes me feel colder than a witch's tit."

"I bet she has a great wee pair of tits just like a wee hot witch."

"Too far, Ringo. Always too far, mate."

"Maybe I should try and hook up with wee Linda. She was a fun girl."

"See if her dog needs a walk."

"No, but really. Maybe if I had been a better boyfriend it could have worked out for us."

"If my aunt had nuts, she would be my uncle. Don't spend your life thinking about ifs, lads."

"Aye, let's get the beers in, boys."

"Sounds good, Ringo."

As the boys were sitting having a beer, Ringo looked up and saw fat Annmarie at the pub door. "What the fuck is she wanting now?"

"Who?"

"Fucking fat Ammo. She has just walked in."

"She better no' come over here with my hangover. Can't deal with her today."

"She is heading this way, lads."

Annmarie walked over to the boys. She had tears in her eyes and was holding something under her jacket. She stood looking at the boys for a second.

"You ok, Ammo, hen?"

"No, I don't think so."

"What you got under your jacket, hen?"

"Nothing."

"Bullshit nothing. What is it?"

"He is gone."

"Who is gone?"

"Del. He is dead."

"What the fuck you talking about?"

"They found him in the Clyde this morning."

"What happened?"

"The police are saying it looks like he killed himself, but I know that's bullshit."

"As Ringo has already asked you, I will ask you too. What's under your jacket?"

"A big fucking knife."

"And who is that for?"

"The Crow. When I find him, I'm going to kill the cunt for killing Del."

"You don't know if he killed him, hen."

"I know and you fucking know it was the Crow, Jagger."

"Don't fucking shout about who killed Del to me, hen. And get that fucking knife away from this table."

"Jagger is right, Ammo. If the Crow finds you, he will kill you too, pal."

"No' if I get him first."

"Right now some cunt will be away to phone the Crow and tell him you are in here talking shit about him."

"Good. Let him come. I will kill him in front of everyone in the pub."

"Take that blade and go and find him. We don't give a fuck."

"If I kill him, I am doing you a favour, Jagger."

"And how do you work that one out?"

"I'm doing what you don't have the balls to do."

"Fuck off, you fat cow."

Annmarie wiped the tears from her face and walked away.

"The cops will find her before the Crow does."

"I hope so, for her sake."

"Do you think she will do it?"

"Hope so."

"I can't believe Del is gone."

"He was a fat junkie, Ringo. Now he is just a dead fat junkie."

"Maybe he did kill himself, knowing that the Crow was going to get him."

"Cunt owes me twenty pounds."

"Owed, Ringo. And you're no' getting that back now."

"What a way to go… jumping into that cold dark water."

"Pushed, you mean."

"Aye, well, either way it's a shit way to end it all."

"It is a shit way. His wee mum will be heartbroken."

"I remember the cunt in school. He was a smelly cunt even back then."

"Aye, he was."

"The story was that his dad would hide his money under the soap and Del would never find it."

"Why would he no' find it?"

"Because he didn't wash, Ringo. For fuck's sake, it was a joke."

"No' a good time to joke, Jagger."

"Fuck him."

"Ok. Now who wants a beer?"

"We all do, Jagger."

"Good. I will get them in then."

As the boys sat and talked about their school days with Del, the pub phone rang and a guy shouted, "Syd, it's for you, mate."

"Who the fuck is that, Syd?"

"How the fuck should I know?"

As Syd walked up to the pub phone, Jagger and Ringo kept talking.

"You know, I used to help Del with his homework back in school."

"Fuck. No wonder he done so bad in life, Ringo."

"Aye, it's my fault."

"Who the fuck is phoning Syd?"

"Fuck knows. Maybe someone looking for a bit of hash."

"Maybe Daisy."

"Doubt it."

"He is worried about something."

"The only cunt that phones me on the pub phone is my mum looking for her dig money."

Syd walked back to the table.

"Is everything all right, Syd?"

"Aye, Jagger, all good. Just my old dear telling me about Del. It must be doing the rounds. Anyway, I need to go."

"Go where?"

"I have things to do, Ringo."

"Like what?"

"Like never fucking mind, that's what."

"It's your round."

"Ok, I will get yous a drink then and when I get back we can go for a curry and a few beers on me, ok, boys?"

Syd got the boys their drinks, put them on the table and said, "Here, lads. I will be back soon. Keep my seat warm, all right? Back in a bit."

Jagger sat watching Syd walk out the pub door. His gut was telling him something was not right. What Jagger didn't know was when you are in a gang of pals there will come a time when you have your last drink together or last laugh or last holiday. It happens right in front of you but you don't know it is happening, like the way you felt as a child on Christmas morning for the last time or the last time you have a beer with your dad. In fact, you might not work out it happened till years later. You will be sitting somewhere having a beer and realise you grew up and you will think, *When was the last time we had a drink together? Where the fuck did everyone go?* But what we know and the boys don't is that this was the last time the three of them would have a beer together in the Argosy. A new chapter was about to start in their lives and time would pull them away from each other like leaves blowing in the wind.

"You ok, Jagger?"

"Aye, Ringo. I just hope Syd is no' doing anything daft."

"Like what?"

"No' sure, mate."

"Maybe he is going to talk to Daisy. You know what he is like."

"Hope that's all."

"He will be fine. Syd is the smart one in the gang."

"I know, but with the cops watching every cunt, just one wrong turn and we could be in the shit."

"Maybe they will pick up the Crow for what happened to Del. Do us all a favour."

"Do you ever get the feeling it's all about to end?"

"Nothing lasts forever, Jagger."

"Aye," Archie added, "We can all have a laugh and a kid on, but our dreams and youth will be gone by dawn."

"Fuck's sake, Archie. That was deep."

"Aye. Morning, Archie."

"Look, lads. I need to tell yous something."

"What's up, mate?"

"Before yous came in, Syd was talking to the Crow."

"About what, Archie?"

"About a job. Something about good money."

"Fucking hell."

"You could have told us sooner, mate."

"He told me to stay out of it, boys. What could I do?"

"What was the job?"

"No' sure. I had just woke up. It was about picking stuff up."

"What, like drugs or money?"

"Both, I think, lads."

"That cunt Crow has a mission to get one of us the fucking jail."

"Aye, but Syd knows that, so why do a job for him?"

"So he can have money to win Daisy back."

"We need to find him."

"It's too late. He will be long gone now."

"So what do we do, Jagger?"

"We wait and hope whatever he is up to, he gets away with it."

"Then what?"

"Then we deal with the Crow."

"We can't win with him, Jagger. He will kill us all, mate. Fucking hell. We will be next to get fished out the river just like Del."

"We need to do something. He is making us look like cunts, Ringo."

"Look, I need to go and pick up some hash. Why don't you go home? I will phone you if I hear anything."

"I'm no' sitting about my flat waiting on bad news."

"Look, maybe Sally has showed up at the flat."

"She can wait."

"But she can't wait, Jagger. That's the problem, mate. She can't wait on you forever."

"Aye, ok, cool. But phone me, Ringo. Good or bad, you phone me."

Jagger walked home thinking about his pal, worried that he would end up in the jail or dead just like Del. He thought, *Del might have been a fat smelly junkie but he didn't deserve that. No cunt deserves to be put in the river on a cold dark night for a shit bag of drugs.* As he got to his close, he saw Leeann sitting on the steps. She looked drunk or stoned.

"You ok, Leeann?"

"I'm fine, Jagger. Just having a minute to myself before I go in."

"You on something? You look like you have had a rough night, pal."

"I have had better nights, Jagger."

"Has the Crow hurt you?"

"No, but him and his goons are no' nice."

"If they have put their hands on you, tell me. I will deal with them."

"It's no' that that's got me upset. It's all this talk about what happened to that guy Del."

"What did they say?"

"No' much but I could hear them laughing. And one of the guys' girlfriends told me it was them who put him in the river last night."

"You need to get away from them. They are all bad news, pal."

"One of them told the girl I was talking to that you are next. The Crow is out to get you."

"Fuck him. He can try."

"No, you don't understand, Jagger. He hasn't done anything to you 'cause the cops have been watching him."

"If he comes for me, we will deal with him and his boyfriends."

"That's just it. He has a plan. I think he wants Syd or Ringo in the jail so then you are all alone."

"If they come for me, I will take him first. His guys won't do anything."

"Maybe you should just get away for a bit. Maybe get Sally and just go away somewhere."

"Look, don't worry, Leeann. Just you stay away from them and look after your mum. Me and the boys will take care of this. It will all be over soon. Just like a bad dream."

"Promise me you won't go looking for him, Jagger. He is dangerous."

"I won't, pal. Now I need to go in. Ringo will be phoning me soon."

Jagger went into his flat, got a beer and sat and waited for the phone to ring. After his first beer he got up for another one. He put the Stones on to pass the time. As an hour went by it felt like a day and still Ringo had not called him. As he went to get another beer, the phone rang.

"Hello?"

"Jagger, it's Ringo."

"Ringo, have you heard from Syd?"

"It's no' good news, mate."

"What happened?"

"You need to chill when I tell you. Don't go nuts, Jagger."

"Ringo, what happened, mate?"

"Syd has been lifted. The cops pulled over the car he was in."

"What did they have in the car?"

"The cops found drugs, money and a hand gun."

"Fucking hell."

"This is just word on the street, mate. It might no' be true."

"It is true. He has been set up."

"Look, Jagger, stay there. I will come to you."

"Aye, cool, Ringo. I'm here, mate."

"Don't go anywhere."

"This is what he wanted. One of us in the jail so we are weak."

"We don't know that, Jagger."

"Yes, we do, Ringo. Yes, we fucking do."

"Look, I will be there soon. Just stay there."

Jagger hung up the phone and went to get his bottle of Jack Daniels out the freezer. He needed a real drink. As he got the bottle out, he only had a bit left in it so he drank it from the bottle. As he put the empty bottle down, he stood in his empty flat and thought about Syd, his poor pal, sitting in a cold empty cell knowing it was all over for him now. He knew Syd was just trying to win the love of his life back. He just wanted money to have a good time with his mates, but now he had nothing and his pals couldn't help him. But they could get revenge for him.

Jagger headed out to get another bottle of Jack. Him and Ringo would need it tonight. He walked to the corner shop and walked right to the back of the shop to get some beers from the fridge. As he was standing looking at the beers, he heard a guy talking to the shop owner, asking about the price of his drink. He knew the guy's voice. As he looked over the shelves, he saw the Crow standing with one of his men.

The Crow told his guy, "You go and get Leeann. Tell her I want her and her wee pals out tonight. We are having a party. Now move."

The guy walked out and Jagger was standing there in the shop, just him, the owner and the Crow. He walked down to the counter where the Crow was asking the guy for cigarettes and a few lucky dips with his carry out.

The Crow told the owner, "I'm feeling lucky tonight, mate." He then turned around to see Jagger standing there. "Well, look who it is."

"You're a fucking grass."

"I'm a grass? And how do you work that out, Jagger?"

"You set Syd up."

"I set him up? What is this? You think I wanted Syd in the jail? He was the only one out of yous three that I liked."

"No, you grass cunts up to the cops so they let you do what you do without going to the jail. You're a shit bag."

"I'm no' a fucking grass and I'm no' a shit bag. You will find out soon, boy."

"You don't look so hard without your guys around, mate."

"I'm no' your fucking mate. Now if you want to do something to stick up for your pal, then go ahead. But you better end me 'cause I will come for you and you won't walk away from it."

The Crow put his money down for his drink and got his change.

The guy in the shop said, "Chill out, lads. I don't need this in here, ok? Pal, what you having?"

"These beers and a bottle of Jack."

The Crow got to the shop door and turned to say, "That Jack to keep you warm in your empty flat, Jagger?"

"No, I might keep it for when Syd gets out and comes looking for you. And he will."

"You think so?"

"Aye. I know and you know why you set Syd up. Because you are shit scared of him. That's why you wanted him out the way."

"The only thing Syd has to worry about just now is how to keep warm in his cold cell. But I'm sure some big guy will give him a nice warm cock up his hole to keep him warm."

Jagger lost his vision a bit with anger. He felt his head spin. His mind went blank. He held onto the counter then grabbed the bottle of Jack and flung it at the Crow. The Crow stood there looking at the bottle going through the air like it was in slow motion. It hit him on the head and Jagger was right behind it. He grabbed the Crow and stuck the nut on him. The Crow fell to the floor.

The guy in the shop was telling Jagger to get out. Jagger looked out the shop window and saw a car coming. Not sure if it was the Crow's boys, he got out the shop and ran down the back streets and into the night. He could hear the Crow shouting from the shop door.

"You're fucking dead, cunt. You hear me?"

Jagger got on a bus into town and got to the first pub that no one would know him. He phoned Ringo to come and meet him and told him, "Make sure no cunt is following you."

Ringo walked into the pub. It was down a lane out the way with not many people in it. "Jagger, why the fuck are we meeting here, mate, and no' the Argosy?"

"I hit the Crow. That's why, Ringo."

"Wait, what the fuck?"

"I know, mate. I didn't think."

"How did this even happen? I told you to stay home."

"Well, I went out to get us a bottle of Jack."

"So where is it?"

"I hit him over the head with it."

"Fucking hell, Jagger. This is bad, mate. So bad."

"Look, I will deal with it."

"How? Tell me how you will deal with the fact that you hit a mad man who has just killed a guy and put our pal away."

"I will, ok? I just need to face him and fight him."

"He won't fight you. He will get his boys to kick the shit out of you then he will fucking stab you as you are helpless on the ground."

"I need to face him. I can't have him coming for my family or you just to get to me. I won't hide from him, Ringo."

"Ok, cool. We will tell cunts what time we will be in the pub and they will show up and we will take them on."

"No. I will show up. You will be out the way, mate."

"Will I fuck. I won't let you face them alone."

"It's me he wants, no' you, so no point the two of us getting a kicking, mate."

"This is fucked up, Jagger. He might kill you."

"Look, if I face him in the pub, he can't kill me and hopefully the cops will show up before he can get to stick a blade in me."

"I don't know about this. Maybe we should just fuck off for a bit."

"No, he will go after Sally or any of our family then to get to me. I need to face the cunt."

"If he kills you and Syd is in the jail, what will I do, mate?"

"I don't know, Ringo, but you always say nothing lasts, all things must pass, mate."

"But I don't want it to end."

"No cunt does."

"Thinking about Syd today and all the stuff we got up to… we have had some good times, Jagger."

"Aye, if we knew back then how good the nineties has been, we would have never have wished our lives away, Ringo."

"So what's the plan then?"

"I need you to head back and tell everyone you meet I will be in the pub tonight at eight o'clock. They should get word of that and I will face the music."

"Ok, I need a drink."

"Aye, me too."

Ringo went to the bar and got two beers and two Jack and Cokes. He took the drinks over to Jagger, held up the Jack and said, "One for the road, mate."

"Aye, one for the road. Cheers, Ringo. You are a good pal."

"A good pal is a guy who knows the meaning of the word pals."

"Some guys have ten pals but sometimes all you need is one good pal, like you, mate."

Later that night Jagger stood across the road from the pub. He was watching everyone coming and going. He didn't see the Crow or any of his guys go in or leave yet but for all he knew they could already be in the pub waiting for him. He stood there knowing that he had to cross the road and go into the pub and face them, but every bit of him was telling him to walk away. He also wanted to make sure that Ringo did not show up because they would go for him too.

He walked over the road and grabbed the handle of the pub door, a thing he had done a million times, but this time could be his last. He took a deep breath, opened the door and walked in. As he walked up to the bar, he looked around. He didn't see the Crow or any of his guys and the pub was not that busy. Probably the word round the camp fire was that shit was going down tonight so a few of the local guys would stay away.

He got to the bar and asked the barmaid for a Jack and Coke.

She asked him, "Do you want ice, Jagger?"

"Yes, please, hen."

"I was told you might show up tonight."

"Talk of the place am I?"

"Aye, you sure you want to be in here tonight?"

"Don't worry about me. Just you get out the way and phone the cops when it kicks off."

"Here, have a double on me."

"Thanks, hen. I might need a few."

A guy walked up behind Jagger and put his hand on his shoulder. Jagger span around. It was Tash and he put his hands up.

"Fucking hell, Tash. You trying to kill me?"

"No, son, but I was told cunts are coming for you in here tonight."

"Aye, don't worry. Just stay out the way, Tash."

"Where is Ringo?"

"No' sure. As long as he is no' here."

"You facing that cunt alone, Jagger?"

"Aye. I need to. No point Ringo getting a kicking."

"Well, good luck, Jagger."

"Thanks, Tash. And if Ringo shows up, Tash, you get a hold of him and keep him out of it."

"He won't like that, Jagger."

"It's no' his fight. It's mine, mate."

"I will try my best, son."

"Cheers."

"You want to sit with me?"

"No' a lot of cunts would ask me that tonight, Tash."

"Well, you are more than welcome to sit with me."

"I will sit with you as long as you move out the way when these cunts show up."

"Aye. Don't worry about that. I will be right out the way of it. I'm too old for fighting."

Tash got Jagger a drink and they sat down at the table. Jagger sipped his Jack and watched the door.

"What time we got, Tash?"

"It's 7:45, son. Why? What time do you think they will show?"

"Any time now, mate."

"You're a brave lad. Don't know if I could sit here and wait for a gang to show up and kick the shit out of me."

"No' my idea of a good time either, mate."

Just as Tash was about to say something to Jagger, the pub door opened. Tash put his hand on Jagger to keep him beside him as the Crow and four of his guys walked in. Jagger told Tash to move away.

"No, son. I can't do that. I'm sitting here with you."

Jagger smiled at Tash and got up and walked over to the bar.

The Crow stood there smiling at Jagger. "I must say I didn't think you would show up, Jagger. You must be a brave cunt."

"Take him yourself, son. Don't be a shit bag."

"You fuck up, old man. This cunt hit me with a fucking bottle. He is getting it and so will you."

"It's fuck all to do with him," Jagger said.

The Crow looked around the pub and said, "Right, anyone who doesn't want to be a part of this, fuck off now."

As a few guys got up and walked out, Jagger walked with them till he was up beside the Crow's men. He pulled out a knuckle duster from his jacket pocket and hit one of the guys right in the chin. The guy dropped to the floor out cold.

"One down," Jagger said as the other three guys went for him.

The three guys grabbed him but he hit one of them in the eye with the duster. The other two guys started punching and kicking him.

The Crow was shouting at them, "Get him fucking down on the ground. Fucking do him."

Other guys in the pub like old Tash were shouting for the guys to leave Jagger alone. Jagger was trying his best to stay up. He knew if they got him down, they could kick him to death. The barmaid was shouting she had phoned the cops. The Crow told her to fuck up. There were a few young girls who were up the back of the pub and were now standing watching in shock.

The Crow shouted at them, "Fuck off back to the pool table. Fuck all to do with yous cows. Now move."

Jagger was still trying to hit the guys back but there was only so much he could take. Just as he was about to fall, old Tash stood up and hit one of the guys over the head with an ash tray. The guy went down but the Crow stepped in and hit old Tash, putting over the table.

As Jagger went to help Tash, the only guy still standing hit Jagger on the back of his head, putting him down on the floor. Jagger was out cold for a few seconds then he opened his eyes. He rolled over and looked around. He saw old Tash on the floor. He was out cold too. As he tried to crawl over to Tash, he saw the Crow walking over to him. Jagger rolled onto his back. The Crow was now standing over him with his hand in his jacket pocket.

The Crow pulled out a blade and, smiling, he said, "You put up a good fight, Jagger. I will give you that, mate."

"Fuck you," Jagger said.

"That was four of my best guys. You done well." Then the Crow bent down and stuck the top of the blade right at Jagger's heart. "I could just slash you, Jagger, but I'm willing to do time for you."

The Crow started to push the blade when Jagger heard a loud bang and the Crow fell over Jagger.

As Jagger pushed the Crow off him, he saw blood on him and the Crow and he looked round to find Ringo standing at the door with his dad's shotgun, smoke still coming out of it.

Jagger said, "Ringo, what the fuck?"

Ringo just stood there for a second then as he lit up a cigarette he said, "Told you it fucking works."

Ringo walked over and grabbed Jagger in his arms. "You ok, mate? Can you walk?"

"Ringo, what the fuck have you done?"

"I had to do it. He was going to kill you, mate."

"Is he dead?"

Ringo kicked the Crow who let out a scream. "No, no' yet."

"You need to get out of here, Ringo."

"No, Jagger. You need to go. The cops are coming for me. No point in me running."

"Then we both stay."

"No, mate. You go. If you can, let them find you another day. Let the cops work for their money."

"You will go away for this, Ringo."

"I'm going away for everything I have done this year anyway, Jagger, so it was best that I done him and no' you."

"Fucking hell, I need a drink."

"I need a port and brandy."

"Or a rub doon with a dead doe."

"You need to get up and go, Jagger, before the cops get here."

"The wee birds over there are eyeing you up with that gun, mate."

"Aye, I know one of them. I have no chance. She is a stuck up wee cow."

"Maybe she will save herself for you, mate."

"No chance. Fucking Moses couldn't part her legs, mate."

"Fuck this, Ringo. I'm staying here, mate."

"Are you fuck, Jagger."

Ringo picked Jagger up and walked him out the pub and shouted to stop a taxi.

"Where the fuck will I go, Ringo?"

"Anywhere but here. Just go and get drunk and out the way. Let me deal with the cops."

"You're a good pal, Ringo. Look after Syd if you see him in the jail."

"I will, Jagger. See you soon, mate."

Jagger got into the taxi and headed off into the night just as the cops drove up to the pub. Ringo stood there watching his pal go as the cops surrounded him. Jagger got the taxi to central station and went to the pub. He got a quick wash in the pub toilets then sat at the bar.

"What you having, mate?" the barman asked him.

"A port and brandy. And a pint, mate."

"Port and brandy together?"

"Aye, please."

"That's a new one, pal. Never been asked that before."

"It's my pal's favourite. Good for when you're having a bad day."

"Must have been some day if you're drinking port and brandy together, pal."

Jagger sat there thinking about his pals who were now both in the cells. He thought about how his gut was telling him something was going to happen. He thought maybe it was all his fault. Then he thought about whether the Crow was still alive or dead. He hoped he was dead.

As Jagger sat there thinking and drinking, Sally walked past going to get the train. She didn't know about anything that had happened today, not yet, and she didn't want to talk to Jagger just now. She was just on her way home from the doctor's and she was not ready to tell him the news she got today. She just stood there looking at Jagger with a tear in her eye and then walked away into the crowd in the train station.

Jagger downed his drinks and walked out the pub and stood looking at the timetable. He thought, *Where to go?* Then he saw Largs and thought with a smile, *Millport. That will do.*

As he walked up to the gate, he saw a few cops kicking about, so he went to walk to another gate and bumped into two CID officers.

"All right, Lucas. Where you off to?"

"My name is no' Lucas, mate. It's Jagger."

"It's fucking Lucas and we need a word with you."

Jagger looked round as the uniform cops surrounded him. "What's the problem, officer?"

"Just need to talk to you down at the station, Lucas. About a fight in the pub you drink in."

"Fuck all to do with me. I have been in town all night."

"Aye? Look, son, I might have been born at night but it wasn't last fucking night."

"I'm telling you I have done fuck all."

"Aye, well, we can talk about that down at the station with your pals David and James or as you call them Ringo and Syd." The cop asked, "What's the deal with the nicknames anyway?"

"We are named after guys in our favourite bands."

"Right, now I get it. Anyway, Lucas, you are under arrest. You do not have to say anything but it may harm your defence if you do not mention when questioned something which you later rely on in court. Anything you do say may be given in evidence." The cops cuffed him. "So do you have anything to say, Jagger?"

"Aye, one word, officer."

"What's that?"

"Smashing."

Printed in Dunstable, United Kingdom